Before Her

Tanishq Maini

ISBN: 9789361287916

An imprint of
tanniiiishq Inc
Mumbai, Maharashtra
India.

To my family, You are the unwavering pillars of my life, the constant source of inspiration.
This book is dedicated to each and every one of you, who has believed in me from the very beginning and encouraged me to chase my dreams.
To my sibling, thank you for being my confidant. Your presence in my life brings joy, laughter, and a sense of camaraderie that fuels my creativity.
To my mentors, thank you for guiding me, challenging me, and pushing me to explore the depths of my abilities. Your wisdom, expertise, and unwavering dedication to my growth have been invaluable.
To the readers and supporters of my novel, thank you for joining me on this enchanting ride. Your engagement, feedback, and appreciation for my work fuel my passion and inspire me to continue on this creative path.
This book is a tribute to the love, encouragement, and unwavering support I have received from each and every one of you. It is a celebration of our shared journey, our shared dreams, and our shared love for the written word.

Contents

Prologue

*In the intricate dance between love, destiny, and the pursuit
of wealth, Liam, a captivating intellect and unparalleled
artisan, weaves a tale of allure and ambition. As the threads
of his character entwine with the dark web's clandestine
offerings, he embraces the forbidden world of illegal weapons,
only to be ensnared in a web of his own making. In the pursuit
of fortune, Liam risks it all, finding himself both puppet
and puppeteer in a symphony of trouble he never foresaw.*

One

In the quiet recesses of his memories, the world before her was a soft symphony of colours waiting for the tender brushstrokes of love to bring vibrancy to his existence. Little did he fathom that destiny had been carefully crafting a masterpiece, and in the convoluted dance of fate, she was poised to step into the frame, transforming the grayscale echoes of his past into a vibrant kaleidoscope of emotions he had yet to discover. His name was Liam Mercer, a man whose days were etched in routine and solitude. A painter by trade, he found solace in the strokes of his brush, each movement a reflection of the unspoken words within his soul. His studio, nestled in the heart of a quaint town, stood as a silent witness to the tales he weaved onto the canvas, The townspeople spoke of Liam in hushed tones, a mysterious figure whose art spoke louder than his words ever could. They marvelled at the way he transformed the ordinary into the extraordinary, infusing a sense of magic into the seemingly mundane. Yet, behind the artistic brilliance lay a man yearning for the hues of passion and the melodies of companionship. One fateful evening, as the amber hues of the setting sun cast long shadows across his studio, Liam felt an inexplicable yearning in the depths of his being. It was as if an unseen force had whispered to him, urging him to venture beyond the familiar strokes of his palette and into the unexplored realms of his own heart. In a nearby café, bathed in the warm glow of hanging lanterns, she sat Ember Reyes, a woman whose laughter echoed like the sweetest melody. Her eyes held the secrets of a thousand stories, and her presence exuded a warmth that could thaw even the coldest of hearts. As Liam entered the café, a gentle breeze seemed to carry the scent of change. The air crackled with an energy that defied explanation, setting the stage for a meeting that would blur the lines between the artist's canvas and the convoluted fabric of existence. Liam strolled into the bustling cafe, an irresistible charm emanating from him. His entrance prompted warm greetings from fellow employees, and with a quick nod, he made his way to the billing centre. Retrieving his order-taking tablet, Liam hurriedly approached the tables, ready to fulfil the late-night orders. As he gracefully navigated through the cafe, his eyes unexpectedly locked onto Ember. Ember, with eyes that were both enchanting and endearing, captured Liam's attention like never before. In that moment, Liam found himself transported to a dreamland of his own creation, where Ember's voice was the sweetest melody. Lost in her presence, he seemed oblivious to the world around him. Ember, noticing Liam's distraction, called over another employee to bring him back to reality. A gentle shake and a few words later, Liam returned, apologising for his momentary lapse. Ember reassured him with a casual smile, "No worries." Liam, eager to make amends, focused on taking their orders, scribbling down the details.

After delivering the orders with finesse, Liam retreated to the pantry. Seated on the floor, he engaged in a friendly banter with a colleague. The teasing took an unexpected turn when the colleague hinted at something more. "Well, do we see something on our way next... huh?"

The mischievous tone hung in the air as Liam blushed noticeably. Attempting to deflect the attention, Liam stammered, "Uh, it's nothing... Can we not talk about it?" The colleague, grinning mischievously, replied, "Yes, we do see her next with you." The air was charged with anticipation, and Liam couldn't help but wonder what the future held for him and Ember. That eve, a spell so rare, to him, a fortune's sweet snare. The morning sun kissed Liam's face as he awoke, his heart brimming with the sweet afterglow of a night he would forever treasure. A radiant smile adorned his lips, a testament to the special connection he shared with Ember. As dawn embraced the world, Liam, the epitome of independence, gracefully rose to greet the day. In the solitude of his home, where the aroma of possibility lingered in the air, Liam decided to prepare a breakfast for one. With no helping hand to assist him, he revelled in the joy of self-sufficiency, a quality that undoubtedly set him apart in the eyes of all the women in the world. He was a man who took charge, unafraid to navigate life's journey on his own. Just as he was engrossed in the quietude of his morning routine, the melodious ring of his phone disrupted the stillness. A message from the café where he toiled as an intern echoed through the receiver, today was a respite from the usual hustle, a day off granted due to a lack of stock to replenish. This unexpected gift of time allowed Liam to immerse himself in his true passion. Seizing the opportunity, he embraced the canvas with fervour, his nimble fingers dancing over the paper like a maestro conducting a symphony.

The subject of his artistic ardour? None other than Ember, the enchanting muse who had captured his heart the night before. In the delicate strokes of his pencil, he etched a draft sketch that mirrored the essence of the unforgettable

Ember. With each stroke of the pencil, Liam lost himself in the memory of Ember's captivating gaze, the way her laughter danced in the air, and the warmth of her presence that lingered in his heart. The sketch began to take shape, capturing not just her physical beauty but the intangible essence that made her unique. As he infused his artistic talent into the portrayal of Ember, the lines on the paper seemed to come alive with the magic of the previous night. Every detail, from the curve of her smile to the sparkle in her eyes, became a testament to the enchantment that had blossomed between them. Liam's hands moved with an almost poetic rhythm, his connection with the sketch transcending the boundaries of mere art. Lost in the creative reverie, Liam felt a familiar warmth spreading within him, a warmth that went beyond the morning sunlight streaming through the window. It was the warmth of newfound emotions, the kind that whispered promises of something more profound than he had ever imagined. With the sketch now complete, Liam stepped back to admire his creation. Ember stared back at him from the paper, her image imbued with an ethereal glow. A sense of satisfaction washed over him, knowing that he had immortalised the magic of their connection in art. The day unfolded like a delicate tapestry, woven with threads of anticipation and the lingering traces of the night before.

Unable to shake off the magnetic pull of Ember's image, Liam decided to take a leisurely stroll through the city, the sketch tucked safely in his pocket. As he wandered the bustling streets, every sight and sound seemed to echo the rhythm of his heart, resonating with the newfound emotions that Ember had awakened within him. The world around him transformed into a romantic backdrop, setting the stage for the blossoming connection he felt with her. As the day melted into evening, Liam found himself standing before the entrance of a charming little bookstore. Drawn by an invisible force, he stepped inside, the soft chime of the bell signalling his arrival. Rows of books lined the shelves, each one whispering tales of love and adventure. Liam's eyes wandered, and there, nestled within the poetry section, he discovered a collection that seemed to call out to him. With a smile, he selected a book of love poems, its pages filled with verses that echoed the sentiments he dared not speak aloud. It was to be a gift, a token of his feelings for Ember. With the book in hand, Liam meandered through the city until he found himself in a quaint park bathed in the soft glow of twilight. Beneath a canopy of trees, he spread out a blanket and sat down, the sketch and the book laid out before him. The evening breeze carried with it the fragrance of blooming flowers, and as the stars began to emerge, Liam couldn't help but feel as though the universe itself was conspiring to weave their story. In that moment, as he traced the lines of Ember's sketch and reflected on the verses within the book, As he waited beneath the starlit sky, Liam couldn't help but wonder how the story of Ember and himself would unfold, and if, just maybe, the universe had conspired to bring two hearts together in a tale as timeless as the love stories that filled the pages of the books surrounding him.

Two

Liam reclined on the soft grass, his eyes fixated on the star-studded night sky, where radiant stars painted a celestial masterpiece. A mild, enchanting breeze whispered through, sending a cascade of shivers through his contemplative reverie. Yet, amid the tranquil beauty, Liam grappled with his own inner demons. His existence seemed tinged with a touch of frustration, burdened by challenges that set his life apart from the ordinary. Beneath the familiar tree, a nightly refuge, he sought solace and answers, his strong exterior hiding the icy depths within his heart. As Liam lay there, surrounded by the quiet beauty of the night, he couldn't escape the tortuous complexities that shadowed his thoughts. The gentle rustle of leaves overhead seemed to echo the whispers of his restless soul. A gentle breeze swept through, causing the leaves to gracefully descend from the tree. Amidst this natural spectacle, one leaf caught Liam's attention, floating delicately through the air. The scene triggered a flood of emotions as memories resurfaced, each leaf carrying the weight of a past incident that haunted him. Liam, already burdened with a fragile heart, was tethered to a regimen of potent medications prescribed by his doctor. His recent struggles had taken a toll on his well-being, manifesting in disrupted sleep patterns and stunted personal growth. In the quiet aftermath of these emotional reflections, Liam rose from his contemplative position and made his way back to the parking lot, where his car patiently waited.

Opening the car door, he embarked on the journey home. One of his cherished comforts was a hidden stash of malt stored in the glovebox, and that night, fortune smiled upon him with the presence of one last bottle. Uncapping it, Liam took a sip, immersing himself in the rich, familiar taste. With the music serenading his solitude, he drove into the night, the amber liquid offering solace to his troubled soul. In the cocoon of his inebriation, Liam navigated the roads with a distant awareness, oblivious to the disapproving symphony of car horns and the chaotic commentary of alarmed onlookers. Unfazed, he continued his journey on the wrong side of the road, a man lost in the depths of his own tumultuous thoughts. As Liam meandered through the labyrinth of his emotions, the city lights blurred into a kaleidoscope of colours, reflecting his inner turmoil. The distant echoes of honking horns and concerned voices gradually faded into the background, drowned out by the melancholy melody playing in his car. In his intoxicated state, Liam found refuge in the warmth of the malt coursing through his veins, a bittersweet elixir that momentarily dulled the sharp edges of his troubles. The rhythmic hum of the engine and the soft crooning of the music created a surreal cocoon around him, shielding him from the harsh reality outside. As he drove aimlessly through the quiet streets, Liam's thoughts swirled like the eddies of a turbulent river. Memories, regrets, and unspoken words intertwined, creating a tapestry of emotions that threatened to consume him. The road ahead seemed endless, much like the journey he found himself on, grappling with the demons that haunted his troubled soul.

In the distance, a faint glimmer of city lights mirrored the tears that welled in Liam's eyes. The weight of his heartache and the intoxication blended into a haze, leaving him suspended in a moment of poignant vulnerability. The world outside his car continued its ceaseless motion, but within, time seemed to stand still. Despite the chaos around him, Liam clung to the solace of the night, the amber glow of streetlights casting a soft radiance on his face. It was a solitary voyage, a journey through the depths of his own heart. Liam drove on, the road ahead uncertain, yet somehow, in that transient space between reality and intoxication, he felt a fragile sense of freedom. Little did he realise that tonight held a chance that would alter the course of his life forever. Cruising down the hushed streets, he found himself losing control of the steering wheel, intoxicated by the alcohol coursing through his veins. Liam's car collided with the mountain, his vision obscured, senses dulled. A deafening honk echoed as his head met the steering wheel with a brutal impact, blood streaming down his forehead. The car door swung open, revealing Ember in the darkness. Liam's forehead was bleeding, and chaos ensued as Ember desperately called for an ambulance. Her phone struggled with signals, adding to the tension. Summoning inner strength, Ember approached Liam's car, acting like a goddess. After multiple attempts, she successfully pulled Liam into her car and rushed him to the hospital, offering reassurance during the drive.

At the hospital, Ember coordinated with the staff to get Liam into surgery.

Waiting anxiously, she maintained her faith. After a tense two hours, the doctors informed Ember that the surgery was successful. She signed the necessary documents, and upon meeting Liam post-surgery, she was surprised to recognize him as the cafe server from that fateful night. In a Hollywood-worthy moment, Ember played the role of a leading lady, swooping in to rescue Liam, creating a scene reminiscent of a romance movie.Their eyes met in the hospital room, a connection forged in the midst of adversity. Ember's heart skipped a beat as she looked at Liam, the man whose life she had just saved. The dim hospital lights cast a soft glow on his face as he smiled gratefully, still recovering from the anaesthesia. "Thank you, Ember," Liam whispered, his voice tender. Ember felt a warm sensation in her chest, realising that this chance encounter had blossomed into something more profound. As the days passed, Ember continued to visit Liam in the hospital. Their conversations deepened, and a bond formed between them that transcended the initial rescue. Ember discovered Liam's passion for art and his dreams of opening a gallery. In turn, Liam learned about Ember's adventurous spirit and her love for literature. Ember's heart fluttered every time she entered the hospital room, and Liam's eyes lit up in her presence. They shared laughter, stories, and dreams, creating a cocoon of intimacy within the sterile hospital walls. After Liam's release from the hospital, Ember insisted on being there for him throughout his recovery. She made a habit of visiting his home almost every day, offering her support and companionship. During these visits, they bonded over shared stories and experiences, deepening their connection. One day, as they were engrossed in conversation, Liam was struck by a sudden realisation. He pulled out a photo of his mother from her childhood, and Ember couldn't help but comment on how adorable she looked. Smiling, she teasingly inquired about the love of his mother's life. Perplexed, Liam was momentarily lost in his own thoughts. Ember, sensing his distraction, playfully asked, "So, where would I find your dad?" His response was a silent admission of an unspoken chaos that left him unable to articulate the complexities of his emotions. As Ember looked at Liam, sensing the unspoken turmoil within him, she decided to gently steer the conversation into a lighter direction. With a warm smile, she said, "You know, family stories can be quite fascinating. Do you have any favourite memories or stories about your parents?" Liam, appreciating her effort to shift the focus, slowly began to share tales of his parents' love and the cherished moments that defined his childhood.

Ember listened intently, offering understanding nods and encouraging him to open up. In the process, they discovered common threads in their family histories, deepening their connection even further. As the day passed, Ember continued to be a constant presence in Liam's life. Their shared laughter, meaningful conversations, and Ember's unwavering support became the pillars of his recovery. Liam found solace in Ember's company, and gradually, the chaos within him began to settle. Out of the blue, the doorbell chimed, surprising Liam as his mother made an unexpected visit after an extended period. Ember called out to Liam, who, upon hearing her, hastened to the door.

As he laid eyes on his mother, a wave of numbness engulfed him, momentarily halting the world around him. Disregarding everything else, he sprinted towards her and embraced her tightly, tears of joy streaming down his face. Ember, quick on her feet, captured a poignant image of the reunited mother-son duo. Gathering his mother's luggage, Liam ushered her into the room. Bewildered by Ember's presence, his mother sought an explanation, and Liam proceeded to recount the situation. His mother, observing them together, remarked, "In harmony you shine, a perfect tether, Side by side, you both look better than ever," causing Liam to blush discreetly, though the telltale signs were evident on his face. Just as the moment settled, the doorbell rang again. This time, Liam's mother took charge, recognizing it as the delivery person. She had a purpose behind her visit, and it was revealed when she unveiled a delectable cake – a birthday surprise for Liam. Ember, caught off guard, inquired about the cake's recipient. His mother disclosed, "It's Liam's birthday today."

Ember found herself in a peculiar moment, realising she had been unaware of Liam's birthday. Despite the unexpected revelation about Liam's birthday, Ember quickly recovered and joined in the celebration. Liam's mother, sensing Ember's surprise, explained that she had planned the surprise visit and birthday celebration to add an extra layer of joy to the reunion. The trio spent the day together, sharing stories, laughter, and the delicious cake. Ember, being an adept photographer, continued to capture candid moments, freezing the essence of the day in images. As the day unfolded, it became a collage of warmth, family bonds, and the joy of unexpected celebrations. In the evening, they decided to dine at Liam's favourite restaurant. The atmosphere was filled with a sense of gratitude and happiness. Ember couldn't help but notice the strong connection between Liam and his mother. It was evident in the way they exchanged glances, the shared laughter, and the unspoken understanding that transcended words. As the night approached, Ember, Liam, and his mother sat together reminiscing about the past and discussing future plans. Liam's mother expressed how proud she was of the person he had become. Ember, still in awe of the surprises the day had brought, realised the significance of capturing not just images but the emotions woven into the fabric of their lives. Ember found herself privileged to witness and document these cherished moments. Little did she know that this day would be etched in her memory as more than just a birthday surprise as it marked the rekindling of family ties.

Three

Liam's childhood revealed a taciturn soul who relished solitude and poured his passion into pursuits like drawing and reciting. Weathering the barbs of others and unjust opposition, life dealt him a tough hand. Despite the community's rejection and efforts to bury his achievements, Liam persevered, paying little heed to the criticisms. Fueled by the belief that he was doing the right thing, he weathered the storm. Realising his late-blooming understanding, Liam embraced the wisdom of learning from his mistakes, evolving into a better person. His mother's persistent encouragement served as a guiding light. Liam acknowledged his past blunders, recognizing life's essence lies in personal growth and learning from missteps. Liam's childhood was marked by adversity and silent endurance, witnessing unpleasant experiences that shaped him. His mother's suffering spurred him to don a resilient smile even in the face of adversity. Witnessing her tears fueled his determination to create a secure life for them both. Facing failures in high school and grappling with despair, Liam refused to succumb to hopelessness. Instead, he embarked on a journey of self-improvement, overcoming obstacles and achieving academic success in his second attempt.

College beckoned, marking a new chapter. Entering his first year, Liam, still reserved, found solace in solitude. During an initial class, his distraction led to a professor's intervention, forcing him to confront his nerves.

Though initially hesitant, Liam surprised everyone with an insightful response, earning praise from the professor. As the day's session concluded, a newfound confidence blossomed within Liam. In the weeks that followed, Liam's transformation continued. His once-muted presence gradually evolved into a quiet confidence that intrigued those around him. The shy demeanour he had carried throughout his life began to thaw as he interacted more with his peers. Beneath the surface, a resilient spirit was awakening. As the semesters unfolded, Liam's academic prowess shone brightly. He not only excelled in his studies but also became a beacon for others who admired his quiet determination. His journey from the shadows of his past to the forefront of success inspired not only admiration but also a growing sense of connection among his classmates. Amidst the academic rigours, Liam found solace in his passion for the arts. Drawing and reciting became not just an escape but a way to express the depths of his soul. Encouraged by newfound friends and a supportive college environment, he started to share his creations, unveiling a hidden talent that had long been veiled. As the seasons changed, so did Liam's life. Liam found himself perusing art pieces in the studio when he heard the soft creak of the door. An alluring girl walked in, immersing herself in the art of crafting. Intrigued by her work, Liam couldn't resist approaching her. "What's this?" he asked. She looked up, a smile playing on her lips, and explained, "It's from Africa, a traditional accessory worn by women." Liam, impressed, remarked, "You seem to know a lot about cultures." She chuckled, replying, "Well, you never know."

As Liam and the girl continued their conversation, their connection deepened. She shared stories of her travels, the vibrant cultures she had encountered, and the significance behind each piece she crafted. Liam found himself captivated not only by her knowledge but also by the passion that radiated from her when she spoke. Days turned into weeks, and Liam eagerly anticipated their encounters in the art room. His fondness for her grew stronger with each passing moment, and it became clear that he had developed feelings for this enchanting girl. However, their budding connection faced an unexpected twist. One day, as they were engrossed in conversation, the girl's phone rang. A sombre expression crossed her face as she answered the call. It was her father, he had received a job transfer, and they were moving to a different city. The news hit Liam like a wave, and a sense of melancholy washed over him. The girl, with a heavy heart, explained the situation. She had to leave abruptly, and there was no time for a proper farewell. Liam tried to mask his disappointment, but the pain lingered in his eyes. As the girl hastily packed her belongings, Liam stood in the art room, watching her leave.

Their connection had been brief but intense, and he felt a void forming as she disappeared from his life. He wanted to express his feelings, but the circumstances didn't allow for a proper goodbye. Liam found solace in the memories of their time together, but the ache of an unfinished story lingered in his heart. Once again, he was left with the bittersweet taste of an unfulfilled story, a longing for a connection that fate had decided to cut short. Liam tried to bury himself in his own art, hoping to find solace in the creative process.

Yet, the colours on his canvas seemed dull, and the inspiration he once drew from their conversations was conspicuously absent. The echo of her laughter and the warmth of her smile lingered in his thoughts, haunting him with the memory of what could have been. In an attempt to cope with the void left by her departure, Liam revisited the African accessory she had introduced him to. Each intricate detail now held a sentimental value, a symbol of the brief but profound connection they had shared. He continued to work on the piece, pouring his emotions into every stroke, as if trying to preserve a fragment of the time they had spent together. Weeks turned into months, and Liam gradually accepted that she was no longer a part of his daily life. The pain dulled, but the memory of her lingered as a bittersweet reminder of a love lost too soon. Life moved on, as it always did. On the day Liam bid farewell to his university after graduation, he embarked on a new journey, seeking employment in a different place. Despite his dedication and hard work, he found himself facing challenges and mistreatment in his job. Realising that the situation wasn't conducive to his well-being, he made the difficult decision to resign, aware of the potential impact on his life, especially as the sole support for his mother. With determination in his heart, Liam packed up and left, saying goodbye once again to his office friends. Undeterred by the twists life threw at him, he refused to give up. Turning his attention to his passion for the arts, he worked night shifts at a restaurant, earning a modest living that he shared with his mother.

Channelling his energy into honing his painting and artistic skills, he also began anonymously reciting poems, showcasing his exceptional talent. In between of these creative pursuits, Liam received an unexpected email from an award company. Initially dismissing it as spam, he couldn't shake the feeling and eventually opened the message. To his astonishment, one of his recited works had been nominated for an award, leaving him in a state of disbelief. Excitement surged through Liam's veins as he absorbed the revelation of his nomination. The initial shock gradually transformed into a burst of euphoria, rekindling a spark of hope that had flickered during the challenging times. The mere idea that his artistic endeavours were recognized on a grand scale filled him with a sense of validation. Unable to contain his elation, Liam shared the news with his mother, who had been a steadfast supporter throughout his tumultuous journey. Her eyes sparkled with pride and joy, recognizing the significance of this unexpected turn of events. Liam found himself immersed in preparations for the award ceremony. The prospect of his work receiving accolades fueled his determination to persevere in the face of adversity. He continued refining his craft, pouring his heart and soul into each stroke of the brush and every carefully crafted word of his poems. The night of the awards ceremony arrived, and Liam, dressed in anticipation and nerves, took the stage. The atmosphere buzzed with excitement as he awaited the announcement. When his name was called, a mixture of disbelief and gratitude washed over him. Stepping forward to accept the award, he couldn't help but feel a surge of triumph, a poignant moment in which he realised that his unwavering dedication to his art had paid off.

The recognition opened doors for Liam, paving the way for opportunities he had only dreamed of. As he continued to thrive in his artistic pursuits, he found a sense of fulfilment that transcended the challenges he had faced. And in the midst of it all, a serendipitous twist awaited, a chance encounter with someone who would play a pivotal role in his personal and creative journey, setting the stage for a new chapter filled with unexpected love and inspiration.

The one who handpicked his creation was the manager of the prestigious award company. She invited Liam to spend the night at the hotel she had arranged, keeping the surprise in store a mystery. Upon entering the room, he discovered his own creation, leaving him bewildered by the unfolding events. As Liam stood there, his eyes fixed on the carefully displayed artwork, a soft glow from the ambient lighting accentuating every detail, he couldn't help but feel a flutter of anticipation and curiosity. The room, adorned with an atmosphere of mystery and romance, seemed to be a canvas of emotions waiting to be explored. The manager, a captivating woman with an air of confidence, stood beside him, watching his reaction with a knowing smile. The connection between them sparked like the subtle flicker of a candle, casting a warm and enchanting glow over the room. As Liam's gaze shifted from the art to her, a silent understanding passed between them. "I wanted you to see your creation in a different light," she said, her voice a melodic whisper that added to the enchantment of the moment. "Art comes to life not only through the strokes of a brush but also in the emotions it evokes."

Liam, still entranced by the beauty surrounding him, felt a surge of gratitude for the unexpected gesture. He began to comprehend that this was not merely about showcasing his artistic talent but an invitation to explore a deeper connection, a connection that transcended the boundaries of canvas and paint. The manager gestured towards a small table adorned with exquisite cuisine, the aroma wafting through the air like a symphony of flavours.

"Tonight is a celebration of your artistry and the emotions it stirs," she continued, her eyes reflecting a warmth that mirrored the ambiance of the room. Liam's heart warmed at the lady's sweet gesture, and a subtle fondness for her began to blossom. Their daily conversations deepened their connection, and as Liam immersed himself in his art at home, he unexpectedly discovered that love had taken root within him. The pair spent hours on calls and engaged in heartfelt video chats, exchanging letters that bridged the gap of their long-distance relationship. However, amidst the enchantment, the bitter reality emerged – Liam, grappling with the pressures of work and home, unknowingly started juggling two relationships. In his misguided attempt to find balance, Liam's actions shattered trust. The intricate web of his double life remained hidden from both women, until guilt weighed heavily on him. Driven by a sense of suffocation, he bravely confessed the truth to both, putting an end to the tangled affair. While regret lingered, Liam vowed not to repeat his mistakes and pledged to embrace honesty in love. Despite the forgiveness of the women involved, Liam couldn't shake the lingering guilt.

Days passed, and he found himself yearning for the unique bond he shared with his manager, reminiscing about the gestures and kindness he had overlooked during his dual dating escapade. Although both women forgave him, Liam still carried the weight of remorse. Despite staying in touch with his manager, unforeseen circumstances led him to withdraw from everyone, choosing a solitary path to self-reflection and personal growth. In his solitude, Liam embarked on a journey of self-discovery and introspection. The echoes of his past actions lingered, serving as a constant reminder of the mistakes he had made. Despite the support of those who forgave him, a sense of loneliness crept into his heart, and he yearned for the warmth of genuine connection. As time passed, Liam found solace in his art, channelling his emotions onto the canvas. Each stroke was a cathartic release, a visual proof to the complex emotions he grappled with. The colours on his palette mirrored the hues of his experiences, the sweetness of newfound love, the bitterness of betrayal, and the deep shades of remorse.

The award manager, sensing his internal struggles, reached out with understanding and compassion. The connection they once shared began to rekindle, like embers reigniting into a comforting flame. Slowly, the wounds of the past started to heal, and Liam found solace in the genuine companionship he had missed. Yet, as life unfolded, unforeseen challenges emerged, and Liam faced a crossroads. The weight of his actions and the ensuing consequences compelled him to make difficult decisions. With a heavy heart, he realised that his journey to redemption required more than artistic expression and rekindled friendships.

It demanded genuine change from within. Liam set out on a path of redemption and growth. The scars of his past remained, but they served as a reminder of the lessons learned. With a newfound commitment to honesty and self-improvement, he vowed to build a future marked by integrity and genuine connection. Love, forgiveness, and personal growth intertwined to shape a narrative that transcended the boundaries of heartbreak, offering hope for a brighter, more authentic tomorrow.

Four

Liam, immersed in showcasing his artistic creations, embarked on international journeys to display his work. During one of these exhibitions, a renowned rapper, whom he deeply admired, discovered one of Liam's masterpieces and expressed interest in purchasing it. Liam, filled with pride, enthusiastically agreed, leading to a joyous celebration with his manager. Returning home, Liam's phone buzzed, revealing a call from his ex-girlfriend at an award show. They engaged in a heartfelt conversation, exploring the complexities of their lives. Despite lingering hopes, their connection couldn't be rekindled, leaving an air of tension. Faced with the unresolved emotions, Liam decided it was time to take a bold step, releasing himself from the past and embracing a fresh start, Liam received an invitation to participate in an exclusive art exhibition that showcased the most promising talents in the industry. The event promised to be a melting pot of creativity and a platform for artists to connect with influential figures in the art world.

As Liam prepared for the exhibition, he couldn't help but reflect on the past and the twists of fate that had brought him to this point. The collision with the famous rapper had opened doors he never imagined, and he felt a renewed sense of purpose in his artistic journey.

The night of the exhibition arrived, and the venue buzzed with excitement. As Liam's artwork garnered attention and admiration, he found himself engaged in conversations with fellow artists, critics, and potential patrons. The atmosphere was charged with creativity and possibility, and Liam felt a sense of belonging within the vibrant art community. The conversations flowed like a river, weaving through various perspectives and interpretations of Liam's work. Each interaction fueled his passion and provided valuable insights that deepened his understanding of his own artistic expression. As the night progressed, a sense of validation and accomplishment settled over Liam. The positive reception from the art community and the genuine interest in his creations affirmed that he was on the right path. He marvelled at the diversity of interpretations his artwork evoked, realising that the beauty of art lay not just in the strokes of the brush but in the myriad ways it resonated with individuals. Amid the bustling crowd, Liam encountered a seasoned art critic who commended his unique approach and innovative concepts. The exchange left him inspired and motivated to explore new horizons in his artistic journey. The critic's words became a catalyst for further introspection, pushing Liam to push the boundaries of his creativity. As the night wore on, patrons and potential buyers expressed their desire to acquire pieces of Liam's collection. The prospect of his art finding homes beyond the exhibition filled him with gratitude and a profound sense of achievement.

It wasn't just about the recognition, it was about sharing a piece of his soul with the world and knowing that it resonated with others. The vibrant energy of the art community enveloped Liam like a comforting embrace. He realised that, in this shared space of creativity, he had discovered kindred spirits who understood the language of art. The connections forged that night extended beyond the boundaries of the exhibition hall, creating a network of support and camaraderie that would continue to inspire and uplift him in his artistic endeavours. As the exhibition drew to a close, Liam stood amidst the echoes of conversations and the lingering scent of possibility. The twists of fate that had led him here now felt like a carefully woven tapestry, each thread contributing to the masterpiece of his life. With a heart brimming with gratitude and a renewed sense of purpose, Liam looked ahead to the future, eager to embark on new artistic adventures fueled by the experiences and connections forged on this remarkable night.

Liam revelled in the joy of his life, despite fleeting thoughts that crossed his mind. Buoyed by happiness, he continued his celebration, and the next day, he proudly purchased his own house and indulged in shopping for luxurious cars. He relished a life he never imagined possible, achieving it through his own efforts, a source of immense pride for both himself and his manager. Embracing a newfound passion for writing, Liam, already skilled in poetry, ventured into penning his own book.

Juggling his creative pursuits with work, he received numerous offers, but selectively took on special projects, basking in the fame he earned in his industry. Decades passed, and Liam's life flourished. He regularly sent financial support to his mother, sharing the success he had worked so hard to achieve. At a formal house party one day, Liam unexpectedly encountered a familiar face, his estranged father. The reunion left him speechless, and as Liam sipped his gin, his father approached, expressing remorse for his shortcomings. Placing a hand on Liam's shoulder, his father apologised for his failings as a father and as a person. In a sudden turn of events, a woman called out to his father, revealing herself as his wife. Liam, in shock, exclaimed, "You can't be serious!" The glass slipped from his intoxicated grasp, shattering on the ground, and he hastily departed. In a haze of emotions, Liam stumbled out of the formal house party, the shattered glass and spilled gin mirroring the fragments of his unexpected encounter with his father. The night air offered little solace as he grappled with the revelation of his father's new life and the years of absence. As Liam walked through the dimly lit streets, memories of his challenging upbringing flooded his mind. He had overcome adversity, rising from a past he never thought he could escape. The newfound success, financial stability, and creative pursuits were his triumphs over the hardships of his youth. However, the sudden reappearance of his father dredged up old wounds and reopened scars he thought had healed.

The following days were a tumultuous whirlwind for Liam. Conflicted between anger, hurt, and a lingering desire for closure, he sought solace in his writing. The pages of his journal became a refuge for his unspoken emotions, a canvas for the turmoil within him. Despite the turmoil, Liam's career continued to flourish. His writing, fueled by the complexity of his emotions, garnered even more attention. The offers poured in, and he carefully selected projects that resonated with his artistic vision. Through it all, he maintained a distant but steady communication with his mother, who remained a pillar of support. As time passed, Liam grappled with the realisation that life's complexities extended beyond his control. The wounds inflicted by his father's absence were not easily healed, and the scars run deep. In moments of vulnerability, he found solace in the creative process, turning his pain into poetry and prose. The day arrived when Liam received an unexpected letter from his father. It was a heartfelt apology, acknowledging the mistakes of the past and expressing a genuine desire for reconciliation. Torn between scepticism and a longing for closure, Liam wrestled with his emotions. Eventually, he agreed to meet his father, setting the stage for a journey of healing and forgiveness. The reunion was both poignant and painful, a collision of past grievances and the tentative hope for a future connection. In the process, Liam discovered the complexity of forgiveness and the transformative power of letting go.

The scars of the past, while indelible, became a proof of resilience and the capacity for growth. As Liam continued his journey, he realised that life's narrative was a tapestry of both joy and sorrow. The encounter with his father, though unexpected, became a chapter of redemption and closure. In the end, Liam found a renewed sense of purpose, not just as a successful writer but as a person who had confronted his past and emerged stronger. Alone, he penned a memoir chronicling his life's journey and the challenges he surmounted. Pursuing his dreams, he transformed adversity into strength, cultivating resilience. Garnering commissions from renowned corporations for his artistic endeavours became a routine, personally delivering each masterpiece. Amidst his flourishing career, he unintentionally neglected the book he authored, garnering rave reviews.

Success trailed in his steps, a pursuit sublime, he wasn't chasing triumph, it was chasing him in rhyme.

As he delved deeper into the demands of his burgeoning career, the pages of his self-written book gathered dust on a neglected shelf. The accolades from readers continued to pour in, yet the very narrative of his own triumphs and tribulations remained a forgotten chapter in his daily hustle.

His artistic endeavours flourished, each stroke of his brush translating into a testament of resilience and determination. The world recognized his talent, and prominent corporations sought his unique touch for their projects. Despite the acclaim and financial rewards, he found himself caught in the whirlwind of deadlines and commitments.

One day, amidst the chaotic symphony of his professional life, a friend stumbled upon his overlooked book. Intrigued by the narrative within, the friend urged him to revisit the pages he had penned in solitude. As he flipped through the forgotten chapters, he realised the profound impact his own story had on others. The words resonated with readers in ways he hadn't anticipated, touching hearts and inspiring those who had faced their own struggles. In the midst of the corporate demands and the constant pursuit of excellence, he rediscovered the essence of his journey. The book, once overshadowed by his artistic success, became a source of renewed purpose. It became a reminder that his journey wasn't just about creating masterpieces for others but also about sharing the raw, unfiltered story of his own battles.

Embracing this realisation, he embarked on a journey of balance. With newfound vigour, he continued to create art for corporate giants, but he also dedicated time to nurture the literary world he had crafted with his own experiences. Success, it seemed, wasn't just about the external accolades it was about the internal satisfaction of staying true to oneself and sharing the wisdom gained along the way.

For weeks on end, Liam found himself unable to reach out to his mother. Faced with a demanding workload, he approached his manager, requesting assistance to convey his apologies and explain that he would be tied up and unable to call her anytime soon. Liam was ensnared in the demands of his job, logging overtime hours that disrupted his sleep pattern and gradually took a toll on his health.

On a near-daily basis, Liam grappled with persistent headaches and backaches, dismissing them as mere inconveniences. One fateful day, amidst his work, he collapsed, prompting immediate concern from his household employees. Alarmed by the sight of Liam unconscious, they urgently summoned a doctor who, upon examination, prescribed medication and insisted he eat without delay. Liam's deteriorating health was a direct consequence of overwhelming work-related stress and an unmanageable workload.

Despite medical advice advocating bed rest, Liam stubbornly persisted in his work, pushing himself to the brink. Alone in his room during a silent night, he experienced severe chest pain. Though a sip of water initially provided relief, the agony returned hours later, with no water left and no viable options. Succumbing to another fainting spell, Liam's fortune took a turn when a returning employee, realising he had left his keys behind, discovered the unconscious figure in the room. Frantically trying to rouse Liam, the employee called for help and, suspecting a more serious issue, swiftly transported him to the hospital. The doctor, observing Liam's profuse sweating, diagnosed him with his first heart stroke, a consequence of unmitigated stress and neglect of precautionary measures. Liam's unconscious body was carefully placed in the doctor's vehicle, and he was promptly driven to the hospital for a thorough examination and treatment.

Upon awakening, Liam was sternly instructed to observe two weeks of bed rest. His manager, prioritising Liam's well-being, refused to let him resume work. Concerned for his son, Liam's mother arrived to care for him during his recovery. Grateful for the support, Liam gradually regained his health and, during this period, requested his manager to distribute the completed statements he had meticulously crafted for various companies. The manager, complying with Liam's request, ensured the timely dissemination of the artwork statements. Taking a hiatus from his demanding work, Liam embarked on a rejuvenating vacation to the enchanting city of Santorini, Greece, marking a well-deserved break after his ordeal. In the picturesque surroundings of Santorini, Liam found solace and healing amidst the breathtaking landscapes and calming waves. The azure waters and vibrant sunsets became his companions, helping him unwind and reflect on the importance of prioritising health over relentless work.

During his vacation, Liam rediscovered the joy of leisurely strolls along the cobblestone streets, indulging in local cuisine, and immersing himself in the rich history and culture of the island. The vibrant colours of Santorini, from the white-washed buildings to the deep blue of the Aegean Sea, provided a therapeutic backdrop for his recovery.

Liam experienced a surge of vitality and purpose, courtesy of a break that allowed him to reevaluate his priorities and commit to achieving a healthier work-life equilibrium.

This interlude acted as a wake-up call, compelling him to prioritise well-being and savour moments of serenity. Returning from Santorini, Liam approached his work with a fresh perspective. Initiating a conversation with his manager, he conveyed his dedication to managing stress and prioritising health. Recognizing Liam's commitment and positive changes, the manager endorsed his decision to embrace a more balanced approach. Liam's time away not only revitalised him physically but also ignited a creative revival. Drawing inspiration from Santorini's beauty, he injected a new, vibrant energy into his artistic pursuits.

The statements Liam had requested his manager to disseminate garnered positive client feedback, affirming the success of his rejuvenated mindset. As Liam progressed in his professional journey, he integrated the lessons from his health scare. Self-care, stress management, and regular breaks became integral components of his daily routine. The Santorini experience marked a pivotal moment, influencing not only his career but also his overall life philosophy. Embracing the transformative power of his Santorini experience, Liam remained steadfast in his commitment to a balanced lifestyle as he navigated his professional journey. The lessons learned from his health scare served as a constant reminder of the significance of self-care and stress management. He began incorporating regular breaks into his routine, fostering a sustainable and fulfilling approach to both work and life.

The positive feedback from clients regarding the completed statements further fueled Liam's passion for infusing creativity into his endeavours. Encouraged by this success, he explored new artistic avenues, continuously seeking inspiration from his surroundings. The vibrant energy he had discovered in Santorini became a driving force behind his innovative projects, marking a distinct phase of creative renaissance in his career. Liam's dedication to maintaining a healthy work-life balance resonated with his colleagues, inspiring a positive shift in the workplace culture. The ripple effect of his transformation extended beyond his own experiences, encouraging others to prioritise well-being and foster a supportive environment.

Five

Liam experienced a profound sense of relief, with a flood of creative ideas streaming into his mind. His first undertaking involved establishing a personal museum, showcasing his multimillion-dollar artworks crafted from extraordinary materials such as Martian remnants and caviar. With determination, he purchased land, initiated construction, and set his plan into motion. In his pursuit of building a grand empire, Liam overlooked the age-old wisdom that impulsive decisions rarely yield favourable outcomes. Despite warnings from his manager about the pitfalls of premature decisions, he remained indifferent and continued to venture into unfamiliar territories without the benefit of experience.As Liam delved deeper into the ambitious project of building his artistic empire, the initial euphoria began to wane. Challenges surfaced, and his lack of expertise in certain areas became increasingly apparent.

The construction faced setbacks, logistical issues arose, and the intricacies of managing a museum demanded skills he hadn't honed. His manager's cautionary advice echoed in the background, a persistent reminder of the wisdom he had chosen to disregard. Yet, Liam pressed on, fueled by the belief in his vision and the allure of success. He remained unfazed by the intricacies of the art world and the complexities of running a museum.

As the construction progressed, financial strains started to manifest. The costly materials and elaborate designs took a toll on Liam's initial budget, putting a strain on the entire project. The warnings he had received seemed prescient, and the reality of hasty decisions began to set in. Liam found himself at a crossroads, facing the consequences of his impulsive actions. The pressure mounted, but he remained determined, attempting to navigate the challenges with a stubborn resolve. It became a test of his resilience and adaptability, as he scrambled to salvage his grand venture.

The once-promising endeavour now hung in the balance, the museum a symbol of both aspiration and recklessness. Liam's journey toward building an empire had become a tumultuous ride, a stark reminder that success often demanded not just vision, but also patience, experience, and a willingness to heed valuable advice. As the construction woes deepened and financial strains tightened their grip, Liam faced the daunting reality of the precarious situation he had created. The grand vision he had initially conceived now teetered on the edge of collapse, a precarious balance between ambition and the pitfalls of impulsive decisions.

The museum, once a beacon of his artistic dreams, became a reflection of the challenges that accompany unchecked ambition. The walls that were supposed to house masterpieces now echoed with the sounds of setbacks and mounting pressure. Liam's journey had evolved into a crucible of adversity, forcing him to reassess his approach and confront the consequences of his hasty decisions.

Undeterred by the storm gathering around his ambitious project, Liam doubled down on his determination.

He sought out experts in the field, attempting to fill the gaps in his knowledge and expertise. Late nights were spent poring over the intricacies of museum management, and he engaged in fervent discussions with seasoned professionals who could provide valuable insights. As the construction delays persisted and the financial strain escalated, Liam found himself at a pivotal juncture. The allure of success still beckoned, but it was now tempered with a newfound humility and a recognition of the importance of heeding wise counsel. The once-dismissed warnings from his manager took on a new significance, and Liam began to appreciate the value of experience in navigating the complex terrain of the art world. In a bid to salvage his grand venture, Liam implemented strategic changes. He sought additional funding, reevaluated the extravagant aspects of the project, and brought in a seasoned team to manage the museum's day-to-day operations. The process was humbling, but it also marked a turning point in Liam's journey.

The once-impulsive visionary now embraced a more measured and informed approach. Liam's ability to learn from his mistakes, pivot when necessary, and persevere in the face of adversity became the defining chapters of his artistic empire. It was a lesson that success, in its truest form, was not just about chasing dreams but also about navigating the challenges with wisdom, patience, and a willingness to evolve.

Liam's empire stood as a symbol not only of his artistic prowess but also of the transformative power of learning from one's missteps. The journey, though tumultuous, had reshaped Liam into a seasoned visionary, a testament to the idea that true success was not just about the destination but also about the transformative journey that led there. As the revamped strategy took root, a subtle but palpable shift occurred within the museum's walls. The once tumultuous construction site transformed into a hive of focused activity. Seasoned professionals collaborated seamlessly, navigating the intricacies of exhibition curation, visitor engagement, and financial management with a newfound cohesion. Liam fostered an environment that encouraged open communication and collaboration, acknowledging the collective expertise of his team. The walls of the museum, once a symbol of struggle, now bore witness to a harmonious blend of creativity and practicality. Liam's journey continued to unfold as the museum finally opened its doors to the public. The once-ambitious visionary now stood humbled by the transformative process. Visitors marvelled at the eclectic collection, not just for its artistic merit but also for the story it told, a narrative of setbacks, adaptation, and eventual triumph. The once-dismissed manager's warnings, now seen as pearls of wisdom, served as a constant reminder of the importance of humility and a willingness to learn. Liam's artistic empire, once on the brink of collapse, now stood as a proof to the transformative power of resilience and adaptability.

It wasn't just a physical space to showcase artwork, it became a living testament to the evolution of a visionary, a beacon for those who dared to dream but understood the importance of navigating the journey with wisdom and humility. As Liam continued to refine and expand his artistic empire, the museum became more than a collection of masterpieces. It became a legacy. Liam had become a versatile individual, though not flawless. His acquired expertise fell short for the domain he navigated, yet he persisted in learning and exerting his utmost effort. Organising a grand event at a museum, he aimed to exhibit his accomplishments and connect with the diverse network he had cultivated. The event, hosted by Liam, unfolded as a significant encounter in which he engaged with various individuals. Amidst the elegant ambiance of the museum. The air buzzed with excitement as attendees, each a thread in the intricate weave of Liam's professional journey, gathered to witness his multifaceted skills. Liam's imperfections only served to humanise him, endearing him to those who appreciated the sincerity of his pursuit for knowledge. As he mingled with the diverse crowd, he exchanged ideas, stories, and insights with people from different walks of life. The museum, a backdrop to this intellectual symphony, echoed with the resonance of shared passions and aspirations. The grandiosity of the event mirrored Liam's commitment to continuous improvement.

It was not merely a showcase of achievements, but a testament to his resilience and willingness to embrace challenges head-on. The connections he had fostered over time converged at this pivotal moment, creating an atmosphere of camaraderie and collaboration.

Throughout the evening, Liam found himself engaged in meaningful conversations, forging new alliances and strengthening existing bonds. The museum, typically a repository of history and artefacts, transformed into a vibrant space where ideas flowed freely, and aspirations took flight. As the event drew to a close, Liam reflected on the myriad interactions that had unfolded. The encounter was more than a networking opportunity, it was a celebration of growth, a recognition of the collective journey undertaken by everyone present. Liam, the imperfect yet relentless learner, had orchestrated an event that transcended its initial purpose, leaving an indelible mark on both his personal and professional odyssey. The event had been a triumph, and Liam found himself elated beyond measure. Grateful for the support he received, he worked tirelessly and celebrated with genuine joy. Once he bid farewell to the guests, Liam returned home. For the first time in his life, he indulged in alcohol. Taking his initial sip, he savoured the taste, gradually consuming the entire drink. Memories from the past flooded his mind, elusive and challenging to grasp. To cope, he poured another shot before retiring to sleep in his formal attire. The alcohol served as a bittersweet elixir, unlocking a cascade of emotions within Liam.

As he reclined in his formal clothes, the weight of the successful event lingered in the air. The room echoed with a subtle silence, disturbed only by the soft rustle of fabric and the occasional clink of the glass against the table. Liam's mind danced between the present triumph and the haunting echoes of bygone days. The alcohol-induced haze acted as a bridge between his accomplished reality and the labyrinth of memories that threatened to engulf him. Each sip brought forth a swirl of emotions, moments of triumph, instances of struggle, and the faces of those who had stood by him.

The room dimly illuminated by a solitary lamp cast shadows that seemed to mirror the juxtaposition of joy and introspection within Liam's soul. He took another measured sip, the amber liquid both a companion and a confidant. The warmth it provided was both physical and emotional, a salve for wounds that time hadn't completely healed. Lost in contemplation, Liam's formal attire felt like a poignant reminder of the expectations and responsibilities that came with success. The fabric clung to him, a tangible reminder of the night's festivities. Yet, as he lay there, a certain vulnerability seeped through the seams of his composed exterior. The clock ticked away, marking the passage of time as Liam's eyelids grew heavy. He succumbed to the alcohol-induced slumber, the events of the night and the memories of yesteryears intermingling in a dreamscape that blurred the lines between celebration and introspection.

In the cocoon of darkness, Liam's dreams became a vivid tapestry, weaving together fragments of his journey.

Scenes from the successful event intermingled with flashes of past struggles and triumphs, creating a surreal landscape of emotions. As the night progressed, Liam's mind navigated through the corridors of nostalgia, revisiting pivotal moments that shaped his identity. Faces of friends and mentors flickered like distant stars, their influence still resonating in the tapestry of his life. The alcohol, a temporary escape, held him in its embrace as dreams unfolded like chapters in a novel. The weight of expectations, the thrill of accomplishments, and the lingering shadows of challenges presented themselves in a kaleidoscope of images.

Each sip had become a catalyst for introspection, unlocking doors to memories long tucked away. In the quietude of his slumber, Liam's subconscious grappled with the paradox of success, the elation that coexisted with the burden of responsibility. The formal attire, once a symbol of achievement, now clung to him like a reminder of the journey's continuous nature. As dawn approached, painting the room with the soft hues of morning, Liam stirred from his alcohol-induced repose. The echoes of the night lingered in his consciousness, leaving him with a sense of clarity and reflection. Slowly, he shed the formal attire that had encapsulated the celebratory spirit, symbolically stepping into a new day, unburdened yet enriched by the experiences of the night. The sunlight streaming through the window heralded a fresh beginning. Liam, now more introspective and attuned to the intricate tapestry of his life, faced the day with renewed vigour. The successful event, the intoxicating sip of alcohol, and the dreams that danced in the night had collectively shaped a chapter of his narrative, propelling him forward into the unwritten pages of his journey.With a gentle awakening, Liam found himself in a room bathed in the soft glow of morning. The remnants of the previous night's revelry lingered like a fading dream. As he rose from his slumber, the events of the successful gathering and the introspective journey fueled by alcohol settled into the recesses of his mind. The formal attire, once donned for celebration, now hung loosely as a symbol of the passing night. Liam moved through the quiet spaces of his home, the echoes of footsteps against the floor carrying a sense of purpose.

The sunlight filtering through the curtains painted warm patterns on the walls, and the promise of a new day unfolded before him. A fresh perspective accompanied Liam as he stepped into the morning light. The weight of the past mingled with the anticipation of the future, creating a harmonious balance that propelled him forward. The celebratory echoes of the successful event still resonated in the air, but now, in the quiet aftermath, Liam felt a renewed sense of purpose. The lessons learned during the night's introspection were etched into his being, guiding him as he faced the challenges and opportunities that lay ahead.

As he ventured into the day, Liam's steps were marked by a newfound confidence, a quiet assurance born from the amalgamation of celebration and reflection. The world outside beckoned, offering a canvas upon which he could paint the next chapter of his journey. The memories of the event, the taste of alcohol, and the dreams that unfolded in the night became threads in the intricate tapestry of his life, each contributing to the evolving narrative.

With a deep breath, Liam embraced the unfolding day, ready to carry the wisdom gained from the night into the uncharted territories of the future. The echoes of success and the subtle traces of introspection walked alongside him, creating a harmonious melody that would accompany him on the continuing journey of his remarkable life. Unbeknownst to him, a mysterious envelope awaited him on the hallway table. The ivory paper and regal wax seal hinted at an unexpected turn of events, injecting an element of intrigue into the aftermath of the celebratory night. Curiosity piqued, Liam gingerly opened the envelope, revealing a letter that seemed to shimmer with an air of enigma. The words on the parchment were carefully chosen, weaving a story that went beyond the boundaries of his recent success. The letter hinted at a hidden chapter in Liam's past, a revelation waiting to be unveiled.

Six

As Liam perused the letter, an unsettling premonition settled over him, suggesting that he stood at the precipice of significant trouble. The words waltzed gracefully across the parchment, weaving a captivating spell of mystery around him. Though the sender chose to remain anonymous, the narrative's familiarity hinted at someone intimately acquainted with the complexities of Liam's life. The missive conveyed a stern warning to Liam, disclosing his involvement in illicit activities. Despite its lack of a signature, the presence of a distinct wax seal hinted at governmental origins. A wave of nervousness and confusion swept over Liam, prompting him to hastily decide to clean up his record. Night after night, as he clandestinely navigated his laptop, Liam had been engaged in the unlawful importation and sale of lethal contraband on the dark web. The government, detecting unusual activity from his IP address, issued a warning through the anonymous letter. Faced with the urgency of the situation, Liam swiftly liquidated his stock of illegal weapons, receiving payment in bitcoins for the transactions. This digital currency's inherent intractability provided him a semblance of safety, leaving the government without concrete evidence to pursue legal action. As Liam meticulously worked to cleanse his record, a sense of urgency and paranoia lingered in the air. Each transaction became a calculated dance between secrecy and profit, his every move shrouded in the shadows of the dark web. Liam knew that time was of the essence, and he couldn't afford any missteps. The government's warning had propelled him into action, pushing him to dismantle his clandestine operation. Night after night, he navigated the intricacies of the digital underworld, ensuring that every trace of his illegal dealings vanished. The bitcoins he received for the weapons provided a layer of anonymity that seemed impenetrable, leaving the authorities with nothing but a cryptic trail. As Liam continued his frenzied efforts to distance himself from his illicit past, the letter's impact lingered in the back of his mind. The anonymous sender had managed to uncover his secret life, leaving him with a profound sense of vulnerability. It was a game of cat and mouse, with the government closing in on the remnants of his activities.

Yet, the world of cryptocurrency provided Liam with a shield against the prying eyes of law enforcement. Bitcoins, being notoriously difficult to trace, offered him a haven in the virtual realm. Each transaction, each transfer of funds, further obscured the paper trail, frustrating any attempts to tie him to the illegal dealings. Despite the intensity of his actions, Liam couldn't shake the feeling that he was being watched. The dance with the government was far from over, and the consequences of his past actions continued to haunt him. As he delved deeper into the world of encrypted transactions and secret negotiations, the line between predator and prey blurred, leaving Liam on the edge of a precipice, unsure of who held the upper hand in this high-stakes game. The nights grew longer, and Liam's paranoia deepened as he meticulously erased any digital footprint that could implicate him. He moved with a cautious precision, aware that a single misstep could tip the scales against him. The looming threat of the government, fueled by the mysterious warning letter, kept him on edge.

In the shadows of the virtual world, Liam found himself entangled in a complex web of deception and evasion. The bitcoins he had earned became both his lifeline and his vulnerability. While their decentralised nature protected him from direct scrutiny, it also left him susceptible to the ever-evolving strategies of law enforcement. As Liam continued to sever ties with his illicit endeavours, he discovered a clandestine community within the dark web, individuals adept at staying one step ahead of government surveillance. He sought their guidance, forging alliances that provided him with valuable insights into the intricate dance between authorities and those operating in the shadows. The government, relentless in its pursuit, intensified its efforts to unveil the elusive figure behind the illegal dealings. Liam, however, remained a ghost in the machine, cleverly manipulating the digital realm to his advantage. His every move became a calculated response to the cat-and-mouse game that unfolded in cyberspace.

The letter, though initially a harbinger of trouble, evolved into a catalyst for Liam's transformation. It forced him to confront the consequences of his actions and adapt to the ever-shifting landscape of the dark web. The line between right and wrong blurred as he navigated through a world where anonymity was both a shield and a sword.

Liam found himself at a crossroads. The government's persistence and his own growing weariness begged the question: could he truly escape the clutches of the digital underworld? The answer remained elusive, shrouded in the uncertainty of a future where every keystroke carried the weight of consequences yet to unfold. With each passing day, Liam's digital odyssey took on a surreal quality, akin to a techno-thriller. The dark web, once his sanctuary, now felt like an unpredictable labyrinth where every node held the potential to expose him. His alliances within the clandestine community provided a fragile sense of security, but trust in this world was a rare commodity. The government, persistent and unyielding, adapted to the elusive nature of Liam's operations. Advanced algorithms and cyber-surveillance tactics became their weapons in this high-stakes game. Liam discovered innovative methods to navigate his financial dealings. He cleverly engaged with NGOs, turning an otherwise troublesome situation into an advantageous one. Despite being under government scrutiny, he maintained a composed demeanour to tackle the issue discreetly. Silently, he sought assistance from an NGO, contributing his illicitly acquired funds as a donation. Subsequently, he proposed the NGO acquire his artistic creations, executing yet another astute manoeuvre to transform his unaccounted wealth into legitimate assets and reap profits. Once again, Liam demonstrated his sharp intellect, employing unconventional means to convert black money into white and emerge victorious. This cunning strategy became a hallmark of Liam's financial dealings. As he delved deeper into this clandestine world, he discovered more intricate ways to navigate the complexities of his transactions. The NGOs, unwittingly serving as his allies, provided both a shield against prying government eyes and a conduit to legitimise his earnings. Liam's static composure in the face of surveillance allowed him to masterfully orchestrate his moves. Aware of the watchful gaze of authorities, he discreetly collaborated with a specific NGO that aligned with his interests. In a clandestine meeting, he shared his predicament and, in a surprising turn of events, donated a substantial amount of his ill-gotten gains to the organisation. The ingenious twist came when Liam proposed that the NGO, now flush with his contribution, acquire his artworks. This not only cleansed his money but also added a layer of legitimacy to his artistic endeavours. The transaction, though illegal in essence, unfolded seamlessly, further solidifying Liam's reputation as a shrewd operator in the shadows. As the NGO obediently acquired his creations, the once black money morphed into white, leaving behind a trail of laundered funds and seemingly legitimate transactions. Liam revelled in the success of his stratagem, enjoying the profits that came from converting his ill-gotten gains into assets that could withstand the scrutiny of even the most discerning financial audits. The cycle continued, with Liam's mind consistently devising new methods to outsmart both the watchful government agencies and potential adversaries in his covert financial manoeuvres. Each move became a calculated step in the intricate dance between legality and deception, solidifying Liam's place as a master manipulator in the clandestine world of financial sorcery. Liam, dissatisfied with his earnings, yearned for more despite his manager's advice against it. Ignoring the cautionary words, he succumbed to his desire and unwittingly set a trap for himself. Abandoning the murky world of dark-web earnings, he dismantled and incinerated his computer. Turning to legal avenues, he ventured into stock trading with a singular goal to amass wealth. Initially, Liam faced a setback, experiencing losses in trading for the first time. Undeterred, he persevered, trading more and eventually turning a profit. However, the newfound wealth failed to satiate his appetite for financial success. Seeking innovative approaches, he leveraged his own museum to enter the IPO arena, selling shares of his company for substantial gains. Utilising his sharp intellect, he reinvested the proceeds back into the market, continuing his pursuit of greater prosperity.

As Liam delved deeper into the realm of IPOs and stock trading, he discovered an insatiable hunger for success within himself. His museum became not just a haven for artefacts but also a strategic asset in his financial pursuits. Leveraging his network and business acumen, Liam strategically timed and orchestrated the release of his company's shares into the market, reaping substantial returns. His shrewd manoeuvres in the stock market continued to yield profits, and Liam's wealth multiplied. Yet, as the numbers in his bank account grew, so did his ambition. Unwilling to rest on his laurels, he sought out new opportunities and investment avenues. Liam became a figure in financial circles, known for his bold strategies and fearless approach. Market fluctuations, economic uncertainties, and the constant need to stay ahead of the curve tested Liam's resilience.

Yet, each setback only fueled his determination to overcome obstacles and emerge victorious. Liam's life became a saga of risk and reward, with every pushing the boundaries of conventional wisdom. As Liam's wealth continued to grow, his desire for fame led him to a bold move,he began publishing news articles and creating sensational headlines that showcased his financial acumen. His calculated manoeuvres and strategic investments became the talk of the town, drawing attention not only from the public but also from government authorities. Caught in the spotlight, government agencies took notice of Liam's extraordinary success. The allure of his wealth raised eyebrows, prompting a thorough investigation into the source of his income. The task fell upon a team of police officers who were assigned to scrutinise Liam's financial affairs. With meticulous inquiry, the officers delved into the details of Liam's earnings, tracing every transaction to unravel the mystery behind his immense wealth. The more they probed, the clearer it became that Liam's financial activities were not as transparent as they seemed. Numerous suspicious transactions were uncovered, pointing towards potential illegitimate means of accumulating wealth. As the investigation unfolded, Liam found himself ensnared in a web of inquiries and allegations. The authorities, armed with evidence of dubious financial dealings, intensified their efforts to expose the truth. The once celebrated figure now faced the scrutiny of law enforcement, and the headlines that once glorified his financial prowess now hinted at a darker side to his success.

Liam's journey, which began with the pursuit of wealth, had taken an unexpected turn. The fame he sought had attracted not only admiration but also the watchful eyes of those tasked with upholding the law. The unfolding investigation would determine whether Liam's rise to prominence was built on legitimate success or if there were darker secrets lurking beneath the surface of his glittering empire. As the investigation deepened, the police officers uncovered a complex web of financial transactions, shell companies, and offshore accounts linked to Liam's wealth. The once elusive success story was now under intense scrutiny, with every financial move being dissected and analysed. Government authorities, determined to get to the bottom of the matter, conducted interviews, examined financial documents, and collaborated with experts to understand the intricacies of Liam's financial empire. It became evident that his wealth was not solely derived from legal avenues, and suspicions of money laundering and tax evasion began to circulate. Liam, feeling the heat of the investigation, tried to maintain an air of innocence. He claimed that his success was the result of astute financial strategies and legitimate investments. However, as the evidence mounted against him, his credibility waned.

The news outlets that once heralded his achievements were now reporting on the investigation.

Liam's reputation took a hit, and public opinion started to shift. The police, armed with a search warrant, raided his home and offices, seizing documents and electronic devices for further examination. Amid the chaos, Liam's once-flourishing empire began to crumble. Stock prices of companies he was associated with plummeted, and investors started pulling out.

Legal battles loomed on the horizon, and the consequences of his actions were catching up with him. As the investigation neared its conclusion, the truth about Liam's financial activities was laid bare. Government authorities were prepared to press charges, and the legal system would now determine the fate of a man who had once soared to great heights fueled by his insatiable appetite for wealth and fame. In the courtroom, Liam faced the consequences of his actions as the legal proceedings unfolded. The evidence presented against him painted a damning picture of financial misconduct, prompting the prosecution to push for charges of money laundering, tax evasion, and securities fraud. Liam's defence team fought vehemently to create doubt, questioning the legitimacy of the evidence and attempting to argue that his financial activities were within legal bounds. The trial became a spectacle, capturing the attention of the public and the media once again. Liam, once the darling of financial circles, now found himself the centre of a high-profile legal battle. As witnesses took the stand and financial experts dissected the intricate details of his transactions, it became increasingly clear that Liam's wealth was built on a foundation of deception. The courtroom drama unfolded like a gripping novel, with each revelation adding a new layer to the complex narrative of his rise and fall. The verdict, eagerly awaited by the public, would determine the fate of a man who had played fast and loose with the boundaries of legality in his pursuit of success. As the judge delivered the sentence, Liam's empire crumbled completely.

He faced substantial fines, asset seizures, and a lengthy prison term for his financial misdeeds. The once-wealthy entrepreneur, now stripped of his fortune and reputation, served as a cautionary tale for those who dared to tread the fine line between ambition and ethical boundaries. The media, which had once chronicled his ascent, now chronicled his downfall, ensuring that Liam's story became a lasting lesson in the perils of unchecked greed. The aftermath of Liam's saga left an indelible mark on the financial world, prompting a reevaluation of regulatory frameworks and increased scrutiny on high-profile individuals. As the public learned from his mistakes, the tale of Liam served as a stark reminder that even the most brilliant minds could not escape the consequences of ethical lapses in the dogged pursual of wealth and fame. While Liam served his prison sentence, the financial world around him underwent significant changes. The fallout from his case prompted increased scrutiny from regulatory bodies and a tightening of loopholes that allowed individuals to exploit the system for personal gain. Liam's former associates faced their own reckoning as investigators delved into their roles in his schemes. Some distanced themselves, attempting to salvage their reputations, while others faced legal consequences for their complicity in the financial wrongdoing. The media continued to follow the aftermath of Liam's downfall, with journalists investigating the broader implications of his actions. The public, once enamoured by his success, now demanded greater transparency and accountability in the business world.

As Liam served his time behind bars, he had ample opportunity for reflection. The consequences of his unyielding quest of wealth and fame had left a lasting impact not only on his life but also on the lives of those connected to him. The prison walls became a crucible of self-discovery, forcing him to confront the choices that had led him down this destructive path.

Seven

Liam found himself sentenced to eight years behind bars, where he grappled with the harsh reality of his actions and the impulsive choices that led him there. Amidst his darkest days in prison, he reflected on the gravity of his mistakes. Meanwhile, his mother anxiously awaited news, clinging to faith during these tumultuous times. Whenever Liam managed to secure a moment for a phone call, he reached out to his mother, seeking solace in their conversations. Her unwavering support became a lifeline for him in the unforgiving confines of prison. As time unfolded, drastic changes occurred: the government seized his assets, stripping him of the luxuries he once enjoyed. Liam's journey became a poignant exploration of redemption, loss, and the enduring strength of maternal love. Behind the cold, unforgiving walls of the prison, Liam faced a daily struggle for self-discovery and redemption. In the solitude of his cell, he delved into the depths of his soul, attempting to untangle the web of decisions that had led him to this point. The passage of time became a relentless companion, marking both the slow erosion of his freedom and the gradual metamorphosis of his perspective. Throughout his incarceration, Liam clung to the lifeline of communication with his mother. Their conversations served as a lifeline, providing a connection to the outside world and a source of comfort in the midst of his tribulations. In the soft cadence of her voice, he found solace, a reminder of the unwavering faith she held in him. On the outside, however, the wheels of change continued to turn. The government, wielding its authority, seized Liam's assets, dismantling the opulent life he once led. The halls that once echoed with the footsteps of affluence were now silent, replaced by the cold echoes of incarceration. As the months turned into years, a subtle transformation occurred within Liam. The crucible of prison forged a tempered resolve, and the flames of remorse burned away the impurities of his past decisions. In the crucible of confinement, he began to piece together a version of himself that was unburdened by the mistakes that had shackled him. In the face of adversity, Liam's mother stood as an emblem of enduring love and unwavering belief. She weathered the storm of her son's incarceration, standing resolute against the winds of despair. Their phone calls became a lifeline that transcended the prison bars, connecting two hearts bound by love and hope.

His mother bore the weight of adversity, a consequence of her son's struggles. Despite the challenges, she toiled tirelessly to carve out a livelihood, securing a humble abode for herself through her relentless efforts. The grind continued, with late-night shifts and hard-earned wages sustaining her. Then, on an ordinary day as she diligently pursued her work, a sudden vibration disrupted the routine. The call was from the hospital, delivering the unsettling news that Liam had been admitted due to a grave health condition. Upon receiving the distressing call, Liam's mother felt her heart skip a beat. Panic and concern surged through her, overpowering the exhaustion from her long day's work. Without wasting a moment, she rushed to the hospital, her mind clouded with worry.

As she arrived at the medical facility, the sterile smell

and the fluorescent lights heightened her anxiety. The receptionist directed her to the ward where Liam was being treated. The journey down the sterile hospital corridor felt endless, each step echoing the drumming of her anxious heart.

Entering the room, she found Liam lying in a hospital bed, his face pale and eyes weary. The sight of her son in such a vulnerable state shook her to the core. The attending doctor explained the severity of Liam's health condition, revealing the complexities of the situation. A knot tightened in her stomach as she absorbed the grim reality. Over the following days, Liam's mother became a constant presence at the hospital, navigating the unfamiliar territory of medical terminology and treatment plans. She juggled her job responsibilities with bedside vigils, the weight of worry etched across her face. Friends and family rallied around, offering support, but the burden of her son's health remained her primary concern. The hospital corridors became a familiar haunt as she shuttled between work and Liam's bedside. The relentless rhythm of hospital life merged with the cadence of her determination. Sleepless nights were spent researching treatments, consulting with specialists, and praying for a breakthrough. In this struggle for her son's well-being, she discovered reserves of strength she never knew existed. The days blurred into a continuous cycle of hope and despair. Liam's condition remained precarious, and the future seemed uncertain.

Yet, amidst the uncertainty, a resilient spirit emerged within her, a mother's unwavering resolve to fight for her child's life. As the days unfolded, the toll on Liam's mother became increasingly evident. The constant juggling between hospital visits, work, and the emotional strain of her son's illness wore her down. Dark circles etched beneath her eyes, and her once vibrant spirit seemed to fade. The weight of the medical bills, coupled with the demands of daily life, pushed her to the brink of exhaustion. Liam, confined to the hospital bed, keenly observed his mother's silent battles. The lines on her face deepened, mirroring the hardships she faced. He longed to reach out, to offer some semblance of comfort or assistance, but his weakened state left him helpless. The realisation of his mother's solitary struggle gnawed at him, and a profound sense of guilt settled in his chest. His attempts to voice his concerns were met with reassurances from his mother, who masked her own vulnerability behind a brave smile. She didn't want to burden him further with the gravity of their situation. Liam, confined to the hospital bed, could only watch as his mother carried the weight of their world on her shoulders. The once lively conversations between them became punctuated by silences filled with unspoken worries. Liam's gratitude for his mother's sacrifices intensified, but so did his frustration at his own incapacity to alleviate her burdens. Days turned into weeks, and the hospital became a stark backdrop to the quiet struggle of a mother sacrificing everything for her child. The absence of a support system became glaringly apparent. Friends and family were sympathetic, but the tangible assistance Liam's mother needed remained elusive. The isolation compounded the hardship, leaving her emotionally drained. Liam, confined to his hospital bed, found solace in the simple act of observing his mother. He admired her strength, her unyielding determination, but he also witnessed the slow erosion of her resilience. It was a poignant paradox,the woman who had always been his pillar of support now teetering on the edge of her own strength. In the quiet moments when their eyes met, Liam could see the weariness in his mother's gaze, a weariness that mirrored the weight of his illness. Yet, in that shared vulnerability, an unspoken bond strengthened between them. Liam's heart ached with the desire to be the source of strength his mother needed, but his frailty confined him to the role of a silent spectator in his own life.

One day, as Liam's mother sat by his bedside, the weariness in her eyes became too apparent to ignore. She sighed deeply, a heavy burden etched on her face, and Liam sensed an unspoken wave of vulnerability washing over her. In that moment, he mustered the strength to speak, his voice weak but filled with concern.

"Mom," he whispered, "I see how much you're going through. I wish I could help."

His mother managed a tender smile, her eyes reflecting both gratitude and sorrow.

"You're already helping by being here, Liam. Your strength is what keeps me going."

Despite her words, Liam couldn't shake the feeling of helplessness that clung to him. He longed to alleviate the strain on his mother's shoulders, to turn the tables and be the caregiver instead of the one in need. The room seemed to close in on him, the confines of the hospital bed a stark reminder of his own physical limitations.

As the days passed, Liam's condition fluctuated, and the reality of their situation loomed larger. His mother, exhausted but resilient, continued her delicate balancing act, managing work, hospital visits, and the emotional rollercoaster of her son's illness. The strain was evident in every movement, in every forced smile, yet she pressed on, refusing to crumble beneath the weight of adversity. Liam, tethered to the hospital bed, grappled with a whirlwind of emotions. He felt a growing admiration for his mother's unwavering dedication, but also an increasing frustration at his inability to contribute. The walls of the hospital room seemed to close in on him, trapping him in a world where he could only observe, unable to offer any tangible support. One evening, as the sun dipped below the horizon and the hospital room was bathed in the soft glow of artificial light, Liam's mother sat beside him. Her tired eyes locked onto his, and he mustered the strength to speak his heart."Mom, I want to be there for you, not just the other way around. I hate feeling so helpless." Tears welled in her eyes as she reached out and gently held his hand. "Liam, you're not helpless. Your presence, your spirit, they mean the world to me. We'll get through this together."

As time progressed, evolving from days to weeks and weeks to months, Liam's condition gradually improved. His mother's unwavering care and the support of the medical team played a pivotal role in his recovery. It was a slow and arduous journey, marked by small victories and setbacks, but eventually, the day came when Liam was deemed well enough to be discharged from the hospital.

Leaving the sterile environment behind, Liam emerged into a world that had changed during his convalescence. His mother, who had been his constant companion through the ordeal, greeted him with tears of joy. The two shared a profound sense of gratitude, a renewed appreciation for the fragile beauty of life. Over the following years, Liam not only regained his physical strength but also embarked on a journey of personal growth and redemption. His experiences in the hospital had left an indelible mark on him, reshaping his priorities and perspectives. With newfound determination, he sought to make amends for the mistakes of his past.

Life, however, had more challenges in store for Liam. The spectre of an eight-year prison sentence loomed over him, a consequence of the choices he had made before his health took a drastic turn. As he faced the legal consequences of his actions, Liam's mother stood by him once again, a pillar of support in the turbulent times ahead. The court hearings were intense, each session a reminder of the past he was desperately trying to leave behind. Legal battles, remorse, and the struggle to rebuild his life outside the hospital walls became his daily reality. Throughout it all, his mother's unwavering belief in his capacity for change fueled his determination to break free from the chains of his past.

The final court hearing marked the culmination of an arduous journey. Liam, now a transformed man, faced the consequences of his actions with a stoic resolve. His mother sat by his side, her support a testament to the bond they had forged through adversity. As the judge pronounced the end of the legal proceedings, a mix of emotions washed over Liam, relief, gratitude, and a deep sense of responsibility for the second chance he had been granted. Upon his release, Liam emerged into a world that looked different from the one he had left behind. He was determined to rebuild his life, make amends for his past, and contribute positively to society. The scars of his journey served as a constant reminder. Liam's reintegration into society was not without its challenges. The stigma of his past actions lingered, casting shadows on his attempts at redemption. However, armed with a newfound sense of purpose and guided by the unwavering support of his mother, Liam committed himself to rebuilding his life from the ground up. The first step was securing employment, a task made more difficult by his criminal record. Undeterred, he approached every opportunity with humility and honesty, determined to prove that he was a changed man. The road was tough, with rejection and scepticism becoming familiar companions, but Liam persisted. Eventually, he found a job that saw beyond his past, offering him a chance to showcase the person he had become. The workplace became a proving ground for his commitment to change, and as he immersed himself in his duties, he began to earn the trust of his colleagues.

Outside of work, Liam embraced opportunities for self-improvement. He attended therapy sessions, seeking to address the root causes of his earlier mistakes and develop healthier coping mechanisms.

Each step forward was a deliberate move away from the person he used to be, and with every passing day, he chipped away at the walls that had once confined him. His mother, a constant source of encouragement, witnessed the transformation with a heart full of pride. She had weathered the storms with him, from the hospital room to the court hearings, and now she saw the fruits of their shared resilience. Their bond, forged in the crucible of adversity, remained unbroken.

<h1 style="text-align:center">Eight</h1>

Liam's journey of recovery was marked by continuous learning, and after several years of dedication and hard work, he radiated success. On a particularly bright morning, he awoke with a sense of accomplishment and set about preparing breakfast for both himself and his mother. Serving her bed tea, Liam engaged in a heartwarming conversation, discussing the challenges his mother had faced during his time in jail. Expressing remorse, he held her hands, kissed them, and vowed not to let her suffer due to his actions again. Determined to be a responsible son, Liam reassured his mother. Amidst this touching moment, his phone buzzed with an email notification, but he chose to ignore it and proceeded to bathe. As he reflected on his past in the shower, feelings of anger and regret washed over him. Hurrying to dress, he checked his phone, only to discover an email with a job offer. Overjoyed, Liam shared the news with his mother, who declared it a propitious day. He revealed that an interview had been scheduled for the same day, prompting him to rush. Despite being pressed for time, Liam forgot to take the medications recommended by his cardiologist, leading to intense anxiety on his way to the interview. As Liam hastily made his way to the job interview, the excitement of the opportunity clashed with the rising anxiety caused by his forgotten medications. The bustling streets and crowded sidewalks seemed to close in on him, amplifying his internal struggle. Each step felt heavier, and the rhythmic beat of his heart echoed louder than usual.

In the middle of the urban chaos, Liam's mind raced, replaying the journey he had taken to reach this point. The rehabilitation, the hard-earned lessons, and the promise he had just made to his mother replayed in his thoughts like a poignant melody. He took a deep breath, attempting to regain composure, reminding himself that this job interview was not only a professional opportunity but also a testament to the progress he had made in rebuilding his life. As he approached the interview location, Liam forced a smile onto his face, determined to leave his anxiety behind and focus on the chance before him. The receptionist greeted him warmly, and he was escorted to the waiting area. In those moments of solitude, Liam found himself reflecting on the resilience that had brought him to this point – a resilience that had, until now, allowed him to overcome every obstacle in his path. When his name was called, Liam entered the interview room with a renewed sense of confidence. The panel of interviewers, seemingly impressed by his resume, greeted him warmly. The conversation flowed smoothly as Liam passionately shared his experiences, skills, and determination to contribute positively to the workplace. He spoke not only of his professional goals but also of the personal growth that had accompanied his journey of recovery. As the interview concluded, Liam left the room feeling a mixture of relief and anticipation. The weight of the past seemed to lift, replaced by a sense of accomplishment. He couldn't help but marvel at the unexpected turn of events that had transformed a morning of anxiety into a day of newfound hope and opportunity. Liam, with a heart full of gratitude and a head held high, looked forward to the possibilities that lay ahead. Exiting the interview room, Liam couldn't shake the elation that accompanied a sense of achievement. The bustling city outside seemed to be in sync with his elevated spirits. He decided to take a moment to call his mother and share the positive outcome. As he dialed her number, he reflected on the transformative power of resilience and the support he had received from his loved ones. His mother's voice on the other end of the line was filled with a mixture of excitement and pride. She offered words of encouragement, reinforcing her belief in his ability to build a better future. Liam felt a surge of gratitude for the unwavering support that had buoyed him through the trials of the past. With the call ended, Liam navigated the city streets, now viewing them through a different lens. The looming skyscrapers seemed to symbolise the heights he could reach, and the vibrant energy of the urban landscape mirrored the newfound optimism within him. While waiting for the job offer confirmation, Liam decided to take a detour to a nearby park. The greenery and peacefulness offered a contrast to the urban hustle, providing him with a moment of introspection. He pondered the significance of the day, recognizing it as a turning point in his life.

Liam felt a renewed sense of responsibility not only to himself but also to those who had stood by him. Liam finally received the long-awaited confirmation for the job offer he had been anticipating. The relief and joy that washed over him, however, came with a twist – the job wasn't located in his hometown but across the country, on another continent altogether, in France. Given that the offer was from a multinational firm with offices worldwide, Liam felt compelled to accept the opportunity, despite the geographical distance. Resigned to starting anew, he agreed to the terms. The recruiting head informed him that his employment would commence early in 2024, and he would receive his tickets to Paris, France, by mail a week before departure.

Leaving the main office, Liam hailed a cab and returned home. Upon entering, he embraced his mother tightly, kissing her on the forehead. Excitement radiated from him as he shared the news. His mother, in turn, advised him, "This time, Liam, you have the chance to make up for lost time, turn your life around, clear your reputation, and find happiness without breaking any laws." In the days leading up to his departure for France, Liam dedicated himself to spending quality time with his mother. They cooked and shared their favourite meals together, reminiscing about old family stories and laughing over cherished memories. Liam took her out to her favourite places in town, ensuring that each outing was filled with joy and warmth.

Recognizing the importance of mending relationships and making amends, Liam reached out to old friends and acquaintances. He rekindled connections, mended bridges, and sought forgiveness from those he may have wronged in the past. The process wasn't always easy, but Liam was determined to start his new chapter with a clean slate.

His mother, a source of unwavering support, offered guidance and encouragement. She reminded him to embrace the opportunity in France as a chance for personal growth and positive change. He had enjoyed quality moments with his dear ones, yet found himself overwhelmed by memories from his past. Despite the emotional challenges, he persevered, steadfastly reminding himself to toil diligently and maintain faith. His motivation wasn't driven by the pursuit of wealth, but rather by the desire to provide his life with countless reasons to thrive and work earnestly. In the wake of his reflections, he realised that the richness of life wasn't measured in dollars earned or fame attained, but in the profound reasons that fueled his determination. Each day became a canvas where he painted the strokes of his resilience and dedication, creating a masterpiece of purpose and meaning. As he navigated the twists and turns of his journey, the echoes of his past served as stepping stones rather than stumbling blocks. They were the reminders of the strength he had discovered within himself, the resilience that had emerged from the crucible of life's trials.

He became a silent warrior, battling not only external challenges but also the internal doubts that occasionally whispered in the corridors of his mind. Through the storms and the calm, he held onto the belief that the true measure of success lay in the pursuit of personal fulfilment and the positive impact he could have on those around him. The pursuit of a life well-lived was his anthem, and the symphony of his efforts played on, resonating with the chords of perseverance and passion. While the world may not have known his name or celebrated his achievements on a grand stage, he found solace in the quiet victories, the daily triumphs over adversity, and the knowledge that his journey was uniquely his own. And so, with each dawn, he embraced the opportunity to write another chapter, not for the applause of the world, but for the quiet satisfaction that comes from living a life true to oneself. Perched on the rooftop, he contemplated life's intricacies. A poetic revelation surfaced in his mind, prompting him to eloquently recite it. Transcribing the verses onto paper, he unwittingly composed a heartfelt ode to his initial love, the woman who first captured his heart, his mother. As the words flowed from his lips, carried by the gentle breeze, he felt a deep connection to the sentiments expressed in his prose. The moon hung in the night sky, casting a soft glow on the city below, and the distant hum of the urban life created a soothing backdrop to his poetic revelation.

Lost in the rhythmic cadence of his own creation, he couldn't help but reminisce about the countless moments his mother had been his guiding light. Each word etched on the paper echoed the gratitude, love, and admiration he felt for her. The rooftop became a stage for his emotions, and the quiet night bore witness to this intimate exchange between a son and his first love. As the last lines of the prose lingered in the air, he gazed up at the stars, feeling a profound sense of connection with the universe. The realisation dawned on him that, in expressing his feelings through his written words, he had not only paid homage to his mother but also unveiled a part of himself that had long been hidden. With a sense of catharsis settling over him, he folded the paper gently and placed it in a small box that he kept as a repository of cherished memories. The rooftop, now a sanctuary of self-discovery, had witnessed the birth of a tribute and the unveiling of emotions that had been silently nurtured over the years. As he descended from the rooftop, the city lights below seemed to twinkle with a newfound warmth. Time flew by, and he found himself just a week away from boarding a flight to France for a work assignment. As he casually browsed through the photos in his phone gallery, the doorbell chimed. To his surprise, it was a registered mail from the company he had recently joined, containing the promised flight tickets. Excitement tingled in the air as he eagerly opened the envelope. The sleek, professionally designed tickets lay within, confirming the reality of his impending journey. The company's attention to detail, evident even in the delivery of the tickets, reassured him about the professionalism he could expect in his new venture. As he traced his finger over the flight details, a surge of anticipation washed over him. It was a mix of both nerves and exhilaration, realising that soon he would be embarking on an adventure in a foreign land. With the tickets in hand, he continued to prepare for the upcoming trip. Packing his bags became a meticulous process, each item carefully chosen to ensure he was ready for both the professional demands of his assignment and the personal experiences he hoped to gather in France. In the midst of the preparations, he couldn't help but reflect on the serendipity of the doorbell's timely ring. The synchronicity of receiving the tickets just as he was mentally gearing up for the journey added a touch of destiny to the unfolding narrative of his life. The week rushed by in a blur of last-minute arrangements and farewells. As the day of departure neared, he felt a mixture of butterflies and a quiet confidence. Armed with his tickets and a suitcase filled with expectations, he was on the brink of a new chapter, a chapter that promised challenges and growth.

On the morning of his departure, the air buzzed with a blend of nervous energy and the promise of new beginnings. The journey to the airport was a kaleidoscope of emotions, with each passing mile bringing him closer to the adventure that awaited him in France. As he stood in line at the check-in counter, the weight of his decision settled in.

It wasn't just about a work assignment, it was about embracing change and venturing into uncharted territory. The airport bustled with people from diverse walks of life, each with their own story and destination. It was a vivid reminder that his own story was about to take an intriguing turn. Passing through security, he found himself gazing out of the airport windows, watching planes taxiing on the runway. The enormity of the skies and the boundless possibilities they represented stirred a sense of awe within him. The world, once confined to the familiar, was now open to exploration. Boarding the plane, he settled into his seat, the hum of the engines signalling the commencement of his journey. As the aircraft ascended into the clouds, he couldn't help but marvel at the vastness below. The landscape transformed beneath him, and with each passing moment, he felt a sense of liberation, as if he were leaving behind the old to embrace the new. During the flight, he perused the work-related materials provided by the company, eager to familiarise himself with the intricacies of the upcoming project. The anticipation of arriving in a foreign country, meeting new colleagues, and immersing himself in a different culture added a layer of excitement to the task at hand. As the plane began its descent into the French landscape, he peered out of the window, greeted by the breathtaking sight of the city lights below.

The realisation that he was about to land in a place where every corner held the potential for discovery filled him with a renewed sense of purpose.

The life adventure had once again officially begun, and as he stepped off the plane onto foreign soil, he carried not just his luggage, but also the anticipation of growth, the thrill of challenges, and the prospect of forging connections that would shape this chapter of his life. The journey was no longer a distant dream but a tangible reality unfolding before him.

Nine

Exiting the airport, Liam promptly booked an online cab and directed the driver to a spot where he could explore apartment rentals. Following Liam's instructions, the cab driver navigated through the city. As Liam scouted for a suitable residence, the majestic Eiffel Tower caught his eye, leaving him in awe. Despite having only seen it through social media and books before, he now had the chance to witness its grandeur in person. Inspired by the iconic landmark, Liam decided to search for apartments online. After a brief search, he stumbled upon a charming unit and shared the location with the cab driver, who skillfully transported him there. Upon reaching the destination, Liam found himself on the 13th floor, gazing at the serene surroundings of his potential new home. However, after negotiations with the owner, he deemed the pricing too high and continued his search. After several attempts, Liam eventually discovered a perfect match that not only felt right but also fit his budget. Thrilled by the prospect of finding his ideal abode, Liam continued his quest for the perfect apartment. The cab weaved through Parisian streets as he explored different neighbourhoods, each holding its unique charm. Along the way, he encountered diverse architectural styles, bustling markets, and quaint cafes that added to the allure of the city.

As the search persisted, Liam's curiosity led him to stumble upon a cosy neighbourhood filled with cobblestone streets and charming boutiques. It felt like a hidden gem waiting to be discovered. Intrigued, he decided to explore the area on foot, discovering a lovely apartment building with a picturesque courtyard. The atmosphere was enchanting, and he couldn't resist inquiring about available units.

After a warm welcome from the building's manager, Liam toured a few apartments, each one offering a distinctive character. Eventually, he found a place that resonated with him – a stylish and comfortable apartment with a view that captured the essence of Paris. Negotiations went smoothly, and Liam secured the rental agreement with a sense of excitement for the new chapter in his life. With the keys to his new apartment in hand, Liam thanked the cab driver for his assistance and set out to explore more of the city. The Eiffel Tower stood tall in the distance, a constant reminder of the unexpected adventure that brought him to this vibrant and captivating place. Little did he know, the journey had just begun, and Paris held countless experiences awaiting him. Embracing the city's enchantment, Liam spent the following days immersing himself in the rich tapestry of Parisian life. He wandered through charming streets, savouring the aroma of freshly baked pastries from corner bakeries and enjoying conversations with locals in quaint cafes.

Liam made the decision to enhance the ambiance of his newly acquired apartment, embarking on a shopping spree to carefully select décor items. He meticulously curated a collection of options to infuse a sense of coziness and aesthetics into his living space. The following morning, he ventured out to procure essential items such as a television, sofa, and other necessities, transforming his room into a haven of beauty and luxury. After dedicating hours to arranging and designing his apartment, Liam succeeded in elevating its aesthetic appeal. As the sun's glow gradually waned, signalling the onset of a new chapter in his life, Liam brewed a cup of coffee and relished the warm weather while marvelling at the view. As darkness descended, Liam prepared a delectable dinner for himself. While dining alone at the table, intrusive thoughts crossed his mind, but he resolved to navigate this journey solo and make his life fulfilling. Following dinner, he reached out to his mother, sharing details about his recent purchases and his impressions of the city. Once the call concluded, Liam continued his evening, savouring solitude. Seeking a breath of fresh air, he stepped onto his balcony, soaking in the nighttime panorama. Lost in contemplation, Liam relaxed and, after an hour, returned to his room, drifting into a peaceful sleep.

The next day, Liam woke up to the gentle rays of the morning sun filtering through his curtains. Energised by a restful night, he decided to explore the neighbourhood and familiarise himself with the local surroundings.

As he strolled through the streets, he discovered quaint cafes, charming parks, and vibrant markets that added character to his new home. Inspired by the discoveries of the day, Liam returned to his apartment with a renewed sense of belonging. He decided to personalise his space further by adding small touches that reflected his personality. He spent the afternoon arranging photo frames, placing potted plants, and selecting artwork that resonated with him. Each addition contributed to the unique atmosphere of his apartment. In the evening, as the sun dipped below the horizon, Liam once again found himself on the balcony, this time with a book in hand. The city lights sparkled in the distance, casting a warm glow over the landscape. Liam savoured the peacefulness of the moment, grateful for the opportunity to create a haven that felt truly his own. Liam gradually settled into his routine. As time passed, Liam continued to find joy in the simple pleasures of daily life. From quiet mornings with a cup of coffee to evenings spent immersed in the city's energy, he embraced the flow of his life. As he stared into the distance, a sense of unease settled over him, knowing that the next day marked the beginning of his new job, the very reason he had come to Paris. After a while, he managed to ease his nerves and meticulously selected a formal attire, ensuring he presented himself in the best light. Returning to his room, he reviewed the company's address, booked a cab, and, with a mind full of thoughts, drifted off to sleep.

The night passed in a blend of anticipation and restlessness.

When the morning light seeped through the curtains, he rose with a mix of excitement and apprehension. As he got ready, he couldn't help but dwell on the significance of this job, the opportunity that had brought him to the vibrant city of Paris. Dressed impeccably, he left his accommodation and hailed a cab, the city awakening with the promise of a new day. The cab ride allowed him a moment to take in the sights of Paris, a city that held both the allure of romance and the weight of professional responsibility. He arrived at the company, a sleek building that mirrored the modernity of his new endeavour. Stepping into the bustling atmosphere of the workplace, he navigated through a sea of faces, each engaged in their tasks. Nervous yet determined, he reported to the designated office where he was greeted by a mix of colleagues and superiors. The day unfolded with introductions, orientations, and a series of tasks that acquainted him with the rhythm of his new professional life. Lunchtime offered a brief respite, and he found himself in a quaint Parisian café, reflecting on the whirlwind of the morning. The taste of espresso lingered on his lips as he contemplated the challenges and opportunities that lay ahead. The afternoon brought a deeper dive into his responsibilities, and he found himself engrossed in the intricacies of his role. As the day progressed, any lingering anxiety began to transform into a sense of purpose and accomplishment.

By the time the workday concluded, he emerged from the office with a newfound confidence, his initial uncertainties replaced by a belief in his abilities. That night, as he strolled through the illuminated streets of Paris, he marvelled at the fusion of his professional journey with the enchantment of the city. The Eiffel Tower stood tall against the night sky, a silent witness to the beginning of a chapter that held both professional growth and personal transformation. In the days that followed, he delved deeper into the intricacies of his new role. The job, which centred around project management and strategic planning, demanded a blend of creativity and analytical acumen. His tasks ranged from developing comprehensive project timelines to collaborating with cross-functional teams, all aimed at achieving the company's ambitious goals. He immersed himself in the challenges, often staying late at the office to ensure he grasped every nuance of his responsibilities. The initial hesitations gave way to a proactive approach, and he quickly earned a reputation for his dedication and attention to detail. In meetings, he spoke with confidence, presenting his ideas and insights with a clarity that resonated with his colleagues and superiors alike. His ability to navigate the corporate landscape became evident as he forged meaningful connections within the company. Networking events and team-building activities provided opportunities for him to showcase not only his professional competence but also his personable nature.

Colleagues admired his collaborative spirit and willingness to go the extra mile to contribute to the success of the projects at hand. As he continued to make strides in his work, he remained conscious of the delicate balance between assertiveness and humility. He sought feedback from mentors and peers, using each piece of advice as a stepping stone for personal and professional growth. His adaptability and openness to learning endeared him to those around him, fostering a positive and collaborative work environment. Beyond the confines of the office, he explored the cultural richness of Paris, attending industry events and networking gatherings. His involvement in the professional community extended beyond the immediate scope of his work, showcasing his commitment to continuous improvement and industry knowledge. Months passed, and his contributions became increasingly indispensable. The initial anxiety that had accompanied his arrival in Paris transformed into a sense of accomplishment. His journey in the city of lights mirrored his professional journey, a fusion of hard work, resilience, and a touch of the magic that only Paris could provide. As the demands of his role intensified, so did the stress and pressure that accompanied it. Liam found himself navigating through a series of unexpected challenges, from tight project deadlines to unforeseen obstacles that tested his problem-solving skills. The weight of responsibility bore down on him, and yet, he met each challenge with a resilience that earned him the respect of his colleagues.

Overtime became a norm for Liam as he poured his energy into ensuring the success of the projects under his purview. Late nights at the office were punctuated by the hum of computers and the glow of city lights filtering through the windows. Despite the fatigue, Liam's determination to deliver excellence never wavered. His leadership abilities came to the forefront during pivotal meetings. As he chaired discussions and presented project updates, he displayed a rare combination of strategic vision and hands-on practicality. His knack for problem-solving shone through, and he adeptly steered the team through complex issues, earning accolades from both his team members and higher-ups. In these meetings, Liam's meticulous preparation and attention to detail were evident. He presented data-driven insights, demonstrating a keen understanding of market trends and project intricacies. His communication skills, honed through countless presentations, ensured that his ideas were not only heard but also well-received. Colleagues began to rely on Liam's expertise, seeking his guidance on critical decisions. The collaborative atmosphere he had fostered within the team became a source of strength during times of high pressure. While the stress persisted, it was met with a sense of camaraderie that transformed challenges into opportunities for growth. Despite the hurdles, Liam remained undeterred. He took calculated risks, implemented innovative solutions, and consistently exceeded expectations.

His ability to thrive under pressure became a defining

aspect of his professional persona. Outside of the boardroom, Liam continued to immerse himself in the cultural fabric of Paris, using the city's energy as both a source of inspiration and a means of rejuvenation. Amid the demanding pace of work, Liam found moments of solace in the charm of Paris. Weekends became a sanctuary, allowing him to explore the city's cobblestone streets, vibrant markets, and iconic landmarks. These moments of respite provided him with the mental clarity needed to face the challenges awaiting him back at the office. The dynamics of his professional life took unexpected turns, presenting opportunities for growth that tested his adaptability. The projects he managed evolved, and with each twist, Liam exhibited a willingness to learn, pivot, and lead his team through uncharted territories. His resilience became a beacon, inspiring those around him to embrace change with a similar spirit. In the midst of high-pressure situations, Liam's leadership style became even more pronounced. He fostered a collaborative environment where every team member felt valued and empowered. As meetings continued to be a platform for decision-making, he encouraged open dialogue and welcomed diverse perspectives. This approach not only strengthened team cohesion but also resulted in innovative solutions that propelled projects forward. Liam's dedication did not go unnoticed by the higher-ups. His exemplary work ethic and ability to navigate complex challenges earned him accolades and, eventually, new responsibilities.

He found himself at the helm of initiatives that stretched his capabilities even further. Despite the increased workload, he met each challenge with a determination that bordered on relentless. The stress, though present, was now accompanied by a sense of achievement. Liam's efforts were rewarded not only in terms of professional recognition but also through the tangible impact he had on the projects he spearheaded. The seeds of success he planted began to bear fruit, and the once-daunting tasks transformed into stepping stones toward his overarching goals. As he continued to steer his professional ship through the ever-changing currents, Liam's story in Paris became one of triumph over adversity. The city, with its timeless elegance and dynamic spirit, served as a backdrop to his personal and professional evolution. As the pace of projects quickened, Liam found himself thrust into a situation where urgency took centre stage. A high-profile presentation loomed on the horizon, a showcase of the myriad activities and projects the company had undertaken under his stewardship. The gravity of the task hit him, and he understood that this presentation would not only encapsulate the essence of their accomplishments but also play a pivotal role in shaping the company's narrative. In the days leading up to the presentation, Liam worked tirelessly. Late nights at the office turned into early mornings as he meticulously compiled data, fine-tuned visuals, and crafted a narrative that seamlessly intertwined the company's achievements with its strategic vision. The pressure was palpable, but Liam thrived in the crucible of urgency, channelling his energy into creating a presentation that would leave a lasting impression. The breadth of activities undertaken by the company became apparent as Liam delved into the details. From successful product launches to groundbreaking partnerships, each slide of the presentation told a story of innovation, collaboration, and measurable success. It was a testament not only to the company's capabilities but also to Liam's adept leadership. In the final stretch, Liam assembled a team of dedicated individuals who shared his commitment to excellence. Together, they refined the presentation, ensuring that every slide reflected the passion and dedication that had fueled their collective efforts. The collaborative spirit within the team reached new heights as they worked in unison to bring forth a narrative that resonated with both precision and authenticity. As the day of the presentation arrived, the energy in the office was charged with anticipation. Liam, now a beacon of calm amidst the storm, stood before the gathered audience and delivered a presentation that captivated and inspired. The visuals spoke volumes, and his articulate narration wove a compelling story of the company's journey under his leadership.The impact was immediate and profound. The presentation garnered accolades from both internal stakeholders and external partners. Liam's adept handling of the material, coupled with the collaborative efforts of his team, elevated the company's standing within the industry. The urgency that had initially weighed on him transformed into a catalyst for a triumph that underscored his ability to excel under pressure. In the aftermath of the presentation, Liam's contributions were acknowledged at various levels of the organisation. His leadership skills, strategic acumen, and capacity to deliver results in challenging circumstances became defining attributes that set him apart.

Ten

Liam consistently burned the midnight oil, yet despite his relentless efforts, recognition eluded him. The late-night toil and the urgent projects and presentations he diligently crafted remained anonymous, with the manager consistently usurping the credit. The manager revelled in a life of luxury, attributing it all to the position he held. However, every story has its conclusion, and this time, the narrative diverged. The manager grappled with severe health issues, prompting Liam to maintain composure and entrust karma with the reckoning. After a few months, higher authorities in the company began acknowledging Liam's contributions.

On an ordinary, radiant day, Liam adhered to his typical routine, grabbing breakfast and heading to the office. Uncharacteristically, he was running late due to his nocturnal work habits. Rushing to his cabin, he promptly reported to senior employees and submitted a drive containing the presentation for the new company project. Relieved after the submission, Liam engaged in casual conversation with his newfound friends among his teammates. Suddenly, his boss summoned him to the office, wearing an expression of anger that left Liam apprehensive, with myriad thoughts racing through his mind.

The boss began by acknowledging Liam's value as an

employee but expressed concern over perceived lack of progress in his assigned tasks, leading to contemplation about his role in the company. Liam, feeling worried, agreed with the assessment but pleaded for another chance, vowing to prioritise and complete the pending work. The boss, seemingly unconvinced, accused Liam of deception, citing evidence that all those presentations were his work. Liam, taken aback, admitted to creating them but explained that he refrained from revealing the truth earlier due to his manager taking credit for his efforts. Expressing disapproval at Liam's silence, the boss, instead of reprimanding him, surprised him with a promotion. Recognizing Liam's exceptional skills, the boss announced that he would now lead the project management team not just in the branch but throughout the entire company. Overwhelmed with happiness and disbelief, Liam shed tears of joy as he realised that his hard work had not only been acknowledged but also rewarded, propelling him to new heights in his professional journey.

Liam, initially blank and incredulous, slowly absorbed the weight of the unexpected news. The promotion was not just a recognition of his talent, but it also symbolised a shift in the trajectory of his career. As the boss outlined the responsibilities and expectations that came with his new role, Liam felt a mix of gratitude and determination.

The news of Liam's promotion spread quickly through the office, generating a buzz of admiration among his colleagues. The same teammates who had become friends were now offering heartfelt congratulations, sharing in his joy.

Liam transitioned into his new position with zeal and a renewed sense of purpose. His leadership style, characterised by fairness and collaboration, quickly garnered respect. Liam's commitment to excellence and his ability to navigate challenges earned him admiration not only from his immediate team but also from other departments within the company. As the head of the project management team, Liam spearheaded successful initiatives, earning accolades from clients and superiors alike. His journey underscored the importance of staying true to one's values and putting in the hard work, even when recognition seemed elusive. Colleagues sought his guidance not only on professional matters but also on navigating the intricacies of office dynamics. Liam remained humble, remembering the challenges he had overcome and the colleagues who had supported him along the way. He became an advocate for acknowledging and appreciating the efforts of every team member, emphasising that success was a collective achievement. In celebration of Liam's promotion, the office decided to host an impromptu evening party to publicly announce the news. The atmosphere was charged with excitement as colleagues gathered in the office, transforming the typically formal workspace into a festive setting.

Decorations adorned the walls, and the hum of animated conversations filled the air as colleagues congratulated Liam on his well-deserved achievement. As the announcement was about to be made, Liam found himself at the centre of attention, surrounded by well-wishers and colleagues eager to toast to his success. The senior management took the stage, highlighting Liam's contributions and expressing confidence in his ability to lead the project management team to new heights. Applause erupted, and the room buzzed with congratulatory cheers. Amidst the jubilation, Liam's eyes met those of an intriguing woman across the room. She exuded an air of confidence and warmth that drew him in. Their eyes locked, creating a magnetic connection that transcended the celebratory chaos. Intrigued, Liam couldn't help but be captivated by her presence. As the evening unfolded, Liam took the opportunity to approach the woman and engage in conversation. It was during this exchange that he discovered she was a new member of the team, having recently joined the company as the Head of the HR department. Her name was Marlowe, and her genuine smile and charismatic demeanour left an indelible impression on Liam. As they continued to converse, Liam found himself unable to divert his attention from Marlowe. The more they spoke, the more he admired her intelligence, humour, and the passion she exhibited for her role. Marlowe, in turn, was equally intrigued by Liam's journey and the resilience that had brought him to this point in his career.

As the night progressed, the revelry continued, and the party transformed into a vibrant celebration of not only Liam's promotion but also the collaborative spirit that defined the company. Colleagues from different departments mingled, forming new connections and strengthening existing bonds. The festive atmosphere, paired with the shared joy of success, created an environment of camaraderie and unity. Later in the evening, during a lighthearted announcement session, it was revealed that Marlowe, the charismatic Head of HR, had played a pivotal role in organising the celebration. Liam couldn't help but feel a sense of gratitude towards her for orchestrating such a memorable evening. The next morning, fueled by a sense of purpose and the energy from the previous night's celebration, Liam wasted no time in getting down to business. As the newly appointed Head of the Project Management team, he set out to implement a series of innovative changes to enhance efficiency and productivity within the company. Liam began by introducing a more transparent communication system, ensuring that the efforts of each team member were acknowledged and celebrated. Regular team meetings were revamped to include open discussions, fostering an environment where ideas flowed freely. Recognizing the importance of collaboration, he encouraged cross-functional teamwork, breaking down silos and promoting a culture of shared success.

In an effort to streamline project management processes, Liam leveraged technology to introduce advanced project tracking and collaboration tools. This not only facilitated real-time communication among team members but also provided valuable insights into project timelines and resource allocation. The newfound efficiency resonated throughout the company, garnering praise from both colleagues and clients. One of Liam's key initiatives was to invest in professional development opportunities for his team. He recognized that a skilled and motivated workforce was essential for the company's sustained success. Training programs, mentorship opportunities, and skill-building workshops were implemented to empower team members and foster a culture of continuous learning. Liam's strategic vision extended beyond the immediate team, as he collaborated with other department heads to optimise cross-functional processes. This holistic approach led to streamlined workflows, faster decision-making, and improved overall company performance. As the positive changes rippled through the organisation, the company began to witness tangible results. Project delivery timelines were met with greater consistency, client satisfaction soared, and the company's reputation for innovation and reliability grew. Liam's leadership style, characterised by empathy and a genuine concern for the well-being of his team, created a positive work environment. Employee morale was at an all-time high, contributing to increased job satisfaction and a notable decrease in turnover.

In recognition of the transformative impact of Liam's leadership, the company's board of directors acknowledged his achievements. They commended his ability to navigate challenges, inspire his team, and drive positive change. As a result, Liam was entrusted with additional responsibilities and given the opportunity to influence company-wide strategies. His journey from the shadows to the forefront of the company's success became an inspiring narrative that resonated not only within the organisation but also in the broader business community. Fueled by his commitment to fairness and transparency, Liam embarked on a mission to ensure that every branch of the company operated under the principles of meritocracy. He visited each branch, holding one-on-one meetings with Project Managers, and delving into the intricacies of their teams' dynamics. During these visits, Liam observed the work environment and listened attentively to the concerns and feedback of both employees and managers. It became apparent that in some branches, there were instances of credit being unfairly taken, hindering the growth and morale of the talented workforce. Liam, armed with the knowledge gained from his visits, identified the individuals responsible for such practices. With a tactful approach, he initiated conversations with those Project Managers who were exploiting the talents of their teams. Liam stressed the importance of acknowledging and rewarding the hard work of every team member. He implemented measures to recognize and rectify the instances where credit was due but not given. In tandem with his efforts to address internal issues, Liam saw an opportunity to revamp the structure of the company's leadership. Recognizing the need for fresh perspectives and expertise, he decided to propose changes during a meeting with the board members. Upon gathering comprehensive insights from his branch visits, Liam scheduled a meeting with the board to discuss crucial factors that could elevate the company's performance. In this meeting, he articulated the need for a strategic overhaul in leadership roles. Liam proposed the addition of fresh members, individuals who could bring diverse skills, perspectives, and a commitment to fostering a positive and collaborative work culture. To implement these changes effectively, Liam urged the board members to seek cooperation from every branch. He emphasised the importance of unity in the company's vision and the need for a cohesive effort to drive sustainable growth. The proposed changes aimed to not only recognize and nurture talent but also to ensure that the company's leadership was aligned with its values of transparency, fairness, and innovation. The board, impressed by Liam's insights and the positive impact he had already made, agreed to support his initiative. Together, they formulated a plan to integrate new members into leadership positions, creating a more dynamic and forward-thinking executive team. The implementation of these changes marked a new chapter for the company, solidifying its commitment to excellence and providing a platform for continued success.

Eager to implement the proposed changes seamlessly, Liam

forged a collaborative partnership with Marlowe, the Head of the HR department. Recognizing that the success of this endeavour depended on identifying and appointing individuals who not only possessed the required skills but also aligned with the company's values, Liam and Marlowe worked closely together. Marlowe's HR team, under her dynamic leadership, collaborated with Liam's project management team to design a comprehensive interview and assessment process. They carefully curated a list of potential candidates, ensuring that each individual's strengths and qualifications matched the specific needs of the branches. The collaborative effort aimed to bring in fresh perspectives and ensure a fair evaluation of every candidate. Late-night strategy sessions became the norm as both teams worked diligently to organise the interviews, evaluations, and subsequent selections. The shared commitment to excellence fueled their determination, and the late-night sessions became a symbol of their collective dedication to the company's success. As the interviews progressed, Marlowe was deeply impressed by Liam's hands-on approach and dedication to creating a merit-based culture within the company. His commitment to fairness and transparency left a lasting impact on her. Marlowe, observing Liam's loyalty towards his team and the broader company vision, found his work ethic and passion for fostering a positive work culture energising.

During one of the late-night planning sessions, Marlowe expressed her admiration for Liam's leadership style. She acknowledged the transformative impact he had already made and shared her enthusiasm for the positive changes that were unfolding within the company. The collaboration between the project management and HR teams exemplified the potential for cross-functional synergy, setting the stage for a more cohesive and collaborative corporate environment. In the midst of the intense planning and execution, a camaraderie developed between Liam and Marlowe. Their shared commitment to organisational excellence and the well-being of the employees fostered a strong working relationship. Marlowe, recognizing Liam's genuine passion for creating a workplace that values its people, found herself inspired to match his dedication. As the selection process concluded, the new leaders seamlessly integrated into their respective branches, bringing a breath of fresh air and injecting new energy into their teams. The collaborative effort between Liam, Marlowe, and their teams had not only reshaped the company's leadership but also reinforced a culture of transparency, meritocracy, and continuous improvement. The late-night endeavours, fueled by shared dedication and a commitment to positive change, laid the foundation for a brighter future for the company. The successful collaboration between Liam and Marlowe became a proof to the transformative power of effective teamwork and visionary leadership. With the newly appointed leaders in place, the company experienced a revitalised sense of purpose and direction. The diverse skill sets and perspectives brought by the fresh leadership infused creativity and innovation into every branch. Teams that had once struggled under inadequate management now thrived with a renewed sense of motivation and support.

Liam continued to lead his project management team with a focus on collaboration and empowerment. Regular feedback sessions and open communication became integral parts of their routine. The positive changes extended beyond the project management department, influencing the entire company culture. Marlowe's HR department played a crucial role in fostering a harmonious work environment. Training programs and mentorship initiatives were expanded to facilitate the professional development of employees at all levels. The efforts made by Marlowe and her team were aimed at nurturing talent and ensuring that every individual felt valued within the organisation.The success of these initiatives became apparent in the company's performance metrics. Projects were executed with greater efficiency, client satisfaction soared, and employee retention rates improved significantly. The positive transformation, once initiated by Liam's determination, had become a collective effort that resonated throughout the entire organisation. Liam and Marlowe, recognizing the need for ongoing improvement, continued to collaborate on various fronts. They organised periodic check-ins to assess the impact of the changes and to identify areas for further enhancement. The bond between them became a symbol of successful cross-departmental cooperation, inspiring other teams to collaborate in pursuit of shared goals. During one of their strategy meetings, Liam and Marlowe discussed the importance of recognizing and celebrating the achievements of employees at all levels. Together, they implemented an employee recognition program that highlighted outstanding contributions and fostered a culture of appreciation. The program not only boosted morale but also reinforced the idea that everyone played a vital role in the company's success. As the company continued to thrive under the new leadership structure, Liam and Marlowe approached the board members with a proposal for a company-wide initiative. Recognizing the importance of employee well-being, they suggested the implementation of comprehensive health and wellness programs. The board, impressed by the results of their collaborative efforts, enthusiastically approved the proposal. The dedication and loyalty displayed by Liam and Marlowe during the transformative period did not go unnoticed. Both leaders were recognized for their exceptional contributions, and Liam's journey from an overlooked employee to a driving force for positive change became an inspirational narrative shared within the company. The success story of Liam, Marlowe, and their teams was not just about organisational growth but also about creating a workplace where individuals could thrive, contribute, and feel valued.

The late-night planning sessions, strategic collaborations, and shared commitment had not only reshaped the company but had also set a precedent for a culture of continuous improvement and collective success.

Eleven

As time passed, Liam's satisfaction with the positive changes in the company deepened. The flourishing branches, the collaborative work culture, and the visible impact on employees' lives were all testaments to the success of his leadership and the collective efforts of the teams. Professionally, Liam had not only reached new heights but had also become a respected figure within the industry.

On a personal level, Liam's journey had also brought about profound changes. The challenges he faced and overcame had shaped him into a stronger, more resilient individual. His commitment to his work became more than just a professional trait, it became a beacon that attracted those around him. Colleagues admired his dedication, and even those outside the company recognized Liam as a leader with unwavering principles. Unbeknownst to Liam, Marlowe had observed his growth and transformation closely. As the Head of HR, she had been a crucial part of the collaborative efforts that had reshaped the company. Over time, she found herself drawn not just to Liam's professional abilities, but also to the qualities that made him who he was. His commitment, integrity, and genuine concern for the well-being of the employees left a lasting impression on Marlowe. Marlowe, too, had grown both personally and professionally alongside Liam.

Their shared dedication to the betterment of the

company created a strong bond between them. She found herself not only admiring Liam's work ethic but also feeling a connection that went beyond the professional realm. Their interactions during meetings, late-night planning sessions, and celebrations had forged a unique camaraderie. It became increasingly evident to Marlowe that her feelings for Liam were evolving. His passion for his work, his ability to inspire those around him, and his unwavering commitment became qualities she valued not just in a professional partner but in a personal one as well. As Marlowe navigated her own journey of self-discovery, she found comfort in the presence of someone who shared her values and aspirations. However, Marlowe remained cautious, as crossing the professional and personal boundaries was a delicate matter. She was aware that the success of their collaboration had been built on trust, respect, and a shared commitment to the company's goals. Marlowe cherished their working relationship and was uncertain whether expressing her feelings would jeopardise the harmony they had created. As Liam and Marlowe continued to lead the company to greater heights, their connection became more apparent to those around them. The unspoken understanding between them was palpable, and colleagues started noticing the chemistry that extended beyond the boardroom. Despite the growing connection between Liam and Marlowe, an unexpected obstacle presented itself.

The company had a stringent policy against personal relationships between colleagues, especially those in leadership roles. Any breach of this policy could result in both of them being removed from their positions. Faced with this challenge, they realised the importance of maintaining professionalism within the workplace.

Determined to navigate this delicate situation, Liam and Marlowe took a cautious approach. Professionally, they remained focused on their roles, ensuring that their commitment to the company's success did not waver. During working hours, their interactions were marked by a strict adherence to company policies and a shared dedication to their responsibilities. Outside the office, however, they found ways to explore their burgeoning connection. As the evenings unfolded, Liam and Marlowe would discreetly transition from their professional personas to individuals seeking to know each other on a personal level. They navigated the intricacies of their newfound feelings, recognizing the need for balance between their personal connection and their roles within the company. To maintain their professional integrity, they chose discreet locations to meet after work. Away from the prying eyes of colleagues, they delved into conversations that revealed more about their backgrounds, interests, and aspirations. Their connection deepened, but they remained acutely aware of the need for discretion. On a personal level, they began to spend time outside of work hours exploring shared interests.

Shopping after work became a routine, providing them with opportunities to laugh, share stories, and create memories that went beyond the confines of the office. Movie nights, dinners, and occasional weekend getaways allowed them to nurture their connection in a private setting. Despite the challenges imposed by company policies, Liam and Marlowe navigated the complexities of their relationship with grace. The need for discretion only intensified the intimacy between them, creating a unique bond that transcended the professional realm. While their roles within the company demanded a level of discretion, the genuine connection they shared allowed them to find joy in the balance they had struck. On a somewhat overcast yet pleasantly warm day, Liam rose from his bed, surrendering to the leisurely pace dictated by the weather. Scrolling through his phone, he noticed a text from Marlowe and engaged in a brief conversation with her before proceeding with his morning routine. After dressing up, he headed out, having rented a car for the week. As Liam embarked on his journey, his phone buzzed once again, revealing Marlowe's caller ID. She informed him that she was running late and requested a ride to the office. In response, Liam accelerated his pace, reaching Marlowe's place swiftly. Stepping out of the car, he graciously opened the door for her, earning a sweet acknowledgment from Marlowe. "How sweet of you, Liam!" she commented as she settled into the car. Without missing a beat, Liam took his place in the driver's seat, and they set off towards the office at a brisk pace. During the drive to the office, the atmosphere inside the car was filled with light banter and shared laughter. Liam and Marlowe effortlessly continued their morning conversation, discussing both work-related matters and casual topics. The comfortable camaraderie between them seemed to make the cloudy day brighter. As they approached the office, Liam expertly navigated through the traffic, ensuring they reached their destination without any delays. Marlowe, appreciating the efficiency and thoughtfulness, expressed her gratitude, "Thanks for the ride, Liam. You really know how to make a morning commute enjoyable." Liam flashed a warm smile, "Anytime, Marlowe. It's my pleasure." He parked the car, and they made their way into the office together. The routine of the day unfolded, with meetings, discussions, and the shared responsibilities that came with their respective roles. Liam dove into his responsibilities as the Head of the Project Management team. Meetings, project reviews, and strategic planning sessions filled his day. His leadership style, marked by efficiency and collaboration, resonated with his team, fostering a productive work environment. Liam's ability to balance assertiveness with approachability earned him the respect and admiration of his colleagues. Throughout the day, he maintained a dynamic approach, addressing challenges with a calm demeanour and providing guidance to his team members. The positive changes initiated by Liam were evident in the improved communication and cohesion within the project management department.

As the workday progressed, Marlowe, too, delved into her responsibilities as the Head of HR. She orchestrated training sessions, addressed employee concerns, and collaborated with other department heads to ensure a harmonious working environment. The collaborative spirit between Liam and Marlowe extended beyond their personal connection and contributed to the overall success of the company. During a break, Liam and Marlowe found a moment to catch up, discussing ongoing projects and potential improvements. In the afternoon, Liam found himself engrossed in a strategy meeting with the board members. His presentation showcased the positive impact of the recent changes in leadership and the resulting improvements in the company's performance. The board acknowledged his efforts, and Liam left the meeting with a sense of accomplishment. As the workday drew to a close, Liam wrapped up his tasks, ensuring that everything was in order for the next day. Marlowe, realising she had no convenient means of transportation to get back home, hesitantly approached Liam. In her mind, the prospect of engaging in a conversation with him during the ride seemed like a welcome opportunity to unwind after the demanding day. In the evening, as they wrapped up their tasks, Liam suggested, "How about grabbing dinner together? A little break from work might be refreshing." Marlowe agreed, and they decided to extend their day beyond the office walls.

Liam decided to treat Marlowe to dinner at a luxurious 7-star hotel. The ambiance was elegant, and the cuisine was nothing short of fabulous. The pair indulged in a delightful dinner, exchanging stories and enjoying the chance to relax after a demanding day at the office. After dinner, as they strolled out of the restaurant, Liam suggested satisfying Marlowe's sweet tooth with some ice cream. The idea resonated with her, and they laughed their way to an ice cream parlour. Liam, aware of Marlowe's fondness for ice cream, was determined to make the evening even more memorable. Diving back into the car, Marlowe noticed that Liam had taken a different route than usual. Confused but curious, she questioned the deviation. Liam, with a mischievous smile, assured her, "We're taking another way." Little did Marlowe know that Liam had planned a surprise ice cream date for her. Arriving at the ice cream parlour, the night was still young, and Liam and Marlowe relished their favourite flavours. The shared laughter, the delicious treats, and the unconventional route home made for an evening that surpassed expectations. As they approached Marlowe's place, she couldn't help but express gratitude for the unexpected detour. Liam, with a twinkle in his eye, suggested that sometimes, taking a different path could lead to delightful surprises. As Marlowe prepared to leave, a lingering moment of hesitation filled the air. With a soft smile, she remarked, "Uh, I shall leave now. Thank you so much for the ice cream. It was a memorable night." Liam, looking into her eyes, responded sincerely, "In this delight, to be by your side was just right." Marlowe smiled warmly, wishing him a goodnight, but both of them sensed there was more to be said. As Liam opened the car's door, he noticed a subtle shift in the atmosphere. He politely asked Marlowe to stop, stepping out of the car himself. With a gentle gesture, he opened the door for her, inviting her to step out just like a queen. Marlowe, feeling a mixture of surprise and delight, graciously stepped out. Standing outside the car, they exchanged their final good-night. Marlowe began walking towards her home, and as she glanced back, she saw Liam looking at her. The unexpected connection led her to turn back towards him. The air was charged with a newfound energy, and in a spontaneous exchange of emotions, they both leaned in and shared a tender kiss. It was an exchange of love that felt both natural and magical. The night concluded on a beautiful note, leaving Liam and Marlowe with a shared sense of warmth and affection. As Marlowe continued her walk home, both of them couldn't shake the feeling that this pleasant night had marked the beginning of something truly special. The spark they felt in those intimate moments lingered, promising the potential for a beautiful journey ahead. As Liam watched Marlowe walk away, the lingering taste of the unexpected kiss lingered on his lips. The air seemed charged with a newfound energy, and a gentle breeze carried with it a sense of joy and warmth. Liam couldn't help but feel a rush of happiness as he got back into the car.

The engine roared to life, and Liam, with a contented smile

on his face, drove back home through the quiet streets illuminated by streetlights. The city seemed to sparkle with a different glow that night, echoing the happiness that resonated within him. The radio played soft tunes, and Liam found himself humming along, lost in the euphoria of the evening. Thoughts of the shared laughter, the intimate moments, and the exchange of affectionate gestures played like a beautiful melody in his mind. As he navigated through the city's winding roads, Liam reflected on the unexpected turn of events. The night had started as a simple drive back home after work, but it had evolved into something far more meaningful. The connection he shared with Marlowe had deepened, and the memory of the shared kiss lingered, leaving an indelible mark on his heart. Arriving at his destination, Liam parked the car and sat there for a moment, relishing the happiness that had enveloped him. The night had not only been pleasant but had opened a door to a new chapter in his life. The prospect of something special with Marlowe filled him with anticipation and a renewed sense of optimism. Entering his home, Liam couldn't shake off the smile that adorned his face. The events of the night replayed in his mind like a cherished film, each scene etching itself into his memory. He felt grateful for the unexpected twists that life sometimes presented and for the connection he had discovered with Marlowe.

As he settled into the quiet of his home, Liam couldn't help but acknowledge the happiness that radiated within him. Liam felt an inexplicable urge to dance. Imagining the moments shared with Marlowe, he twirled around his living room, his heart filled with a rhythm of bliss. In the midst of his euphoria, Liam decided to revisit the magical evening through the pictures he had unknowingly taken of Marlowe. Excitedly, he reached for his phone, only to realise with a hint of disappointment that it had no battery left. Unfazed, he plugged his phone into the charging, blissfully unaware of the messages that awaited him. Minutes later, as his phone gained a little charge, it flickered back to life. To his surprise, the screen lit up with a flurry of notifications, all from Marlowe. She had spammed him with texts, expressing concern about his well-being and eagerly awaiting his response. Realising the oversight, Liam quickly scrolled through Marlowe's messages, witnessing the transformation from excitement to worry in her words. Concerned about him reaching home safely, Marlowe had become increasingly anxious with each unanswered text. Determined to reassure her, Liam wasted no time. As soon as his phone became reachable, Marlowe promptly made a call. Liam could sense the mix of relief and mild irritation in her voice as she asked, "Are you fine?" Marlowe expressed her frustration at not receiving a prompt response, revealing just how much she cared. Apologising for the unintentional delay, Liam explained the battery mishap and the whirlwind of happiness that had temporarily distracted him. Marlowe, realising his genuine enthusiasm, couldn't help but chuckle at the situation. Liam's ability to turn a potentially worrisome moment into a lighthearted one brought a smile back to her face. As they continued talking, the laughter turned into more intimate conversations. Liam and Marlowe found themselves sharing thoughts, dreams, and aspirations, losing track of time. The gentle cadence of their voices became a lullaby, and before they knew it, the night had transitioned into the early hours of the morning. In the comfort of their respective spaces, Liam and Marlowe decided to go to sleep while still connected through the phone call. The tender exchanges and shared laughter created a bridge between their worlds. The night had been more than just an exchange of gestures, it had been a celebration of connection, shared moments, and the promise of something beautiful on the horizon.

Twelve

Liam and Marlowe embarked on their usual daily routines, each immersed in their respective responsibilities at the office. The day seemed ordinary until an announcement circulated, bringing a wave of joy. Selected employees were granted a vacation due to the office undergoing renovations. While some colleagues eagerly packed their workstations for a break, Liam and Marlowe found themselves dedicated to their roles as their office expanded, requiring the appointment of new team members. Despite the allure of a holiday, Liam and Marlowe remained committed to their tasks. As their colleagues left for a well-deserved break, the two of them stayed behind, working late into the night. The office, usually bustling with activity, now echoed only with the sound of Liam and Marlowe's diligent efforts. One evening, as they toiled in the quiet office, Liam noticed Marlowe stretching wearily. Concerned for her well-being, he approached her to offer some companionship. Engaging in conversation, Liam gently touched Marlowe, who felt a mix of intimidation and attraction. Marlowe expressed her concern about being observed, but Liam reassured her with a playful shout, confirming that they were alone. In a bold move, Liam kissed Marlowe passionately, igniting a fire between them. The atmosphere became charged with desire as Liam explored Marlowe's lips and neck, evoking a range of emotions from her. The intensity of the moment led

Marlowe to confess her love for Liam. Embracing the passion, Liam lifted Marlowe onto a nearby table, his hands exploring her body. In the throes of passion, Liam undressed Marlowe, creating an intimate connection between them. The office, once filled with the hum of productivity, now resonated with the sounds of their shared pleasure. Marlowe's moans intertwined with Liam's desire, creating an atmosphere of intense intimacy. Their entwined bodies and the symphony of their desire painted a picture of unrestrained passion. The night became a canvas for their love, leaving them both breathless and satiated, wrapped in the aftermath of their intense intimacy. The profound connection forged during that passionate night marked a turning point in Liam and Marlowe's relationship. As the days passed, the intensity of their feelings only deepened. Recognizing the strength of their bond, they made a decision that would further intertwine their lives – Marlowe moved into Liam's home. Their shared commitment and the desire for an even deeper connection propelled them forward. Marlowe's belongings found a place alongside Liam's. Liam and Marlowe navigated the challenges and joys of cohabitation. From morning routines to late-night conversations, they discovered the nuances of each other's habits and quirks. The once solitary spaces now echoed with shared laughter, quiet moments, and the echoes of their growing love. Liam's home became a canvas for their shared life.

The kitchen witnessed collaborative cooking sessions, where they explored new recipes and created dishes infused with love. Every corner of the house seemed to resonate with the warmth of their affection. Their days were punctuated with shared responsibilities and moments of leisure. The evenings were a celebration of their love story. Whether it was watching movies, enjoying home-cooked dinners, or simply basking in the comfort of each other's presence, Liam and Marlowe found solace in the simplicity of shared moments. Their connection, once confined to the office space, now flourished in the intimacy of their home. Liam and Marlowe continued to learn about each other, unveiling layers of their personalities. Communication became the cornerstone of their relationship, allowing them to express their needs, desires, and dreams. Each day brought them closer, creating a sanctuary where their love could thrive. The decision for Marlowe to move in with Liam was not just about cohabitation, it symbolised a shared commitment to building a life together. Their home became a proof to the beauty of love, messy, imperfect, and incredibly fulfilling.

The rhythm of Liam and Marlowe's shared life resonated with the comforting cadence of love. In their domestic haven, Marlowe took on the role of an enchanting chef, creating culinary wonders that filled their home with tantalising aromas. Each meal she prepared was a labour of love, a gesture that spoke volumes about the depth of their connection.

Liam, in turn, appreciated Marlowe's culinary prowess. The dining table became a stage where they indulged in delicious feasts, sharing not just the food but also the warmth of their shared moments. The kitchen, once a solitary space, now echoed with laughter and the clinking of utensils, a symphony of their togetherness. Their evenings were adorned with a comforting routine. After a day of work, they would unwind in each other's company, relishing the peacefulness of their shared space. The simple act of being together, whether engrossed in conversation or quietly enjoying each other's presence, became a cherished part of their daily lives. Commuting to the office took on a new charm as they embarked on this journey together. The shared car rides were filled with playful banter, shared dreams, and the occasional stolen glances that spoke volumes. The once mundane routine of heading to work transformed into an adventure, with each journey becoming an opportunity to deepen their connection. As the months unfolded, Liam harboured a delightful secret to express his profound love for Marlowe. One day, he surprised her with a brand new car, a symbol of their shared journey and a testament to the joy he found in her companionship. The gleaming vehicle stood as a tangible manifestation of Liam's appreciation for the happiness Marlowe brought into his life. Marlowe, touched by the thoughtful gesture, was overwhelmed with emotion. The surprise not only represented a material gift but also encapsulated the love and dedication Liam felt for her. The new car became a vessel for their shared adventures, symbolising the exciting journeys they would embark on together. With their lives now intricately woven together. The much-anticipated day arrived when Liam and Marlowe were not only recognized for their exceptional efforts but were also rewarded with a well-deserved vacation. The board members, impressed by their unwavering dedication and outstanding performances, decided to express their gratitude by granting them time off. In a meeting filled with praise and acknowledgment, Liam found himself at the centre of attention. The board members commended his tireless efforts in steering the company through its expansion phase. Marlowe's invaluable contributions were also highlighted, and their collaborative spirit was lauded as a driving force behind the company's success. The joyous news of the vacation brought an extra layer of excitement to their lives. The duo decided to embark on an adventure to Poland, a destination that held promises of culture, history, and landscapes. Liam and Marlowe's journey through Poland unfolded like a storybook, each page filled with new experiences and cherished memories. They started their exploration in the historic city of Warsaw, immersing themselves in the rich tapestry of Poland's capital. The cobbled streets and grand architecture whispered tales of the city's past, leaving Liam and Marlowe captivated. As they wandered through the Royal Castle and the picturesque Old Town, the couple couldn't help but marvel at the resilience of Warsaw, which had risen from the ashes of war to become a symbol of strength and resilience. The memories of the city's cultural richness and historical significance lingered with them long after they moved on. Their next stop was Krakow, a city known for its mediaeval charm and vibrant atmosphere. The magnificent Wawel Castle and the enchanting Market Square became the backdrop for romantic strolls and shared laughter. Liam and Marlowe indulged in the local cuisine, savouring pierogi and kielbasa, creating gastronomic memories that would stay with them forever. The journey continued to Zakopane, a mountain resort nestled in the Tatra Mountains. Surrounded by breathtaking landscapes, Liam and Marlowe embarked on hikes, breathing in the crisp mountain air. The peacefulness of the region provided the perfect setting for moments of quiet reflection and shared dreams. Their adventures took an unexpected turn as they explored the off-beat location of Bialowieza Forest, home to the last and largest primaeval forest in Europe. Liam and Marlowe marvelled at the ancient oaks and elusive European bison, forging a connection with nature that left an indelible mark on their souls. The couple's Polish odyssey reached its crescendo in Gdansk, a coastal city with a rich maritime history. Walking hand in hand along the Baltic Sea, they were drawn to the iconic Long Market and the historic shipyard, where the Solidarity movement had taken root. The spirit of resilience and the quest for freedom left a profound impact on Liam and Marlowe. As they boarded a cruise to explore the Baltic Sea, Liam and Marlowe discovered the allure of the water, the gentle sway of the ship echoing the rhythm of their hearts. The cruise became a floating haven of shared moments, filled with sunsets, starlit nights, and the magic of the open sea. In the glow of sunsets and the serenity of dawn, Liam and Marlowe found solace in each other's company. Their Polish adventure concluded with a return to Warsaw, where they reflected on the multitude of experiences that had shaped their journey. The memories they carried away were not just captured in photographs but etched into the very fabric of their relationship. The vacation wasn't just a break from work, it was a celebration of their achievements, a recognition of their dedication, and an opportunity to revel in the joy of love. Liam and Marlowe returned to their daily lives with hearts full of gratitude for the shared moments that had transformed their vacation into a celebration. Upon returning to their home in Paris, the city of love, Liam and Marlowe found themselves enchanted by the familiar yet timeless allure of the Eiffel Tower. The iconic landmark, standing tall against the Parisian skyline, beckoned them with a promise of romantic moments under the shimmering city lights. As night descended, casting a magical glow over the city, Liam and Marlowe decided to spend a memorable evening beneath the Eiffel Tower. The gentle hum of the city and the distant melodies of street musicians created an ambiance of unparalleled romance. Under the graceful arches of the iconic monument, Liam and Marlowe found a quiet spot to savour the beauty of the Parisian night. The Eiffel Tower, adorned with sparkling lights, became a majestic backdrop to their shared moments. The city below seemed to hush into a gentle murmur, allowing the couple to immerse themselves in the magic of the moment. Wrapped in the warm glow of the Eiffel Tower's lights, Liam and Marlowe engaged in heartfelt conversations, reliving the memories of their Polish adventure. The soft breeze carried with it the whispers of their dreams, and the night unfolded as a canvas painted with the hues of love. As they stood together, hand in hand, beneath the iconic structure, Liam and Marlowe exchanged promises and expressions of affection. The city of Paris, known for its romantic charm, provided the perfect setting for a quiet celebration of their journey, a testament to the enduring beauty of their love. The Eiffel Tower, standing tall like a guardian of romance, bore witness to the couple's quiet moments of reflection, laughter, and shared dreams.As the night unfolded under the watchful gaze of the Eiffel Tower, Liam and Marlowe felt the exhilaration of the moment take hold of them. The crisp night air enveloped them, adding a touch of chill to the atmosphere, yet their hearts remained warm with the shared joy of being in each other's company. Drawn to the enchanting melody of distant music, the couple decided to let spontaneity guide their steps. With the Eiffel Tower as their ethereal backdrop, Liam and Marlowe swayed to the rhythm of their own love story. The twinkling lights of Paris above mirrored the stars that adorned the night sky, creating a celestial dance floor just for them. The cold weather seemed to fade away as the couple embraced the dance of romance. Marlowe, with a radiant smile, twirled under the open sky, her laughter harmonising with the melodies of the night. Liam, equally caught up in the magic of the moment, led her in graceful spins and twirls, their movements echoing the timeless romance that Paris exuded. Under the canvas of stars, with the Eiffel Tower standing tall as a silent witness to their dance, Liam and Marlowe found solace in the intimacy of their shared steps. The cold breeze brushed against their faces, but the warmth of their connection kindled a fire within. In the quietude of the night, they waltzed under the open sky, creating memories that would forever be etched in the tapestry of their love story. The celestial dance continued, with the couple losing themselves in the sheer magic of the moment. Their laughter echoed through the empty spaces, and the city lights flickered in harmony with their every step. The cold weather became an afterthought as the heat of their love radiated, creating an atmosphere where time seemed to stand still. As the dance concluded, Liam and Marlowe stood beneath the Eiffel Tower, their breath visible in the cold night air. The stars above bore witness to a love that had transcended the ordinary, a dance that spoke of shared dreams and the promise of forever. Hand in hand, they strolled away, leaving behind the celestial dance floor, their hearts brimming with the magic of the starlit night in the city of love. After their enchanting dance beneath the starlit night, Liam and Marlowe decided to extend their magical evening with a leisurely stroll along the charming streets of Paris. The city, bathed in the soft glow of streetlights, exuded a romantic ambiance that only Paris could offer. They meandered through the historic neighbourhoods, their footsteps echoing on cobblestone pathways, as if the city itself was applauding their love. As they walked hand in hand, the night, filled with a subtle chill, encouraged them to draw closer. The warmth they shared became a comforting shield against the cold, creating an intimate cocoon that cocooned them in the heart of the city of love. Paris, with its timeless allure, seemed to embrace them with open arms. They explored hidden corners and secret alcoves, where the whispers of centuries past mingled with the soft rustling of leaves overhead. Each step revealed a new facet of the city's charm, and Liam and Marlowe savoured the beauty of their surroundings. Finding a quiet spot with a view of the Seine River, they settled down. The lights of the city reflected on the water's surface, creating a shimmering tapestry that mirrored the romance of the night. With a gentle breeze playing with their hair, they threw stones into the river, their laughter merging with the soothing sounds of the flowing water. As they sat by the Seine, Liam and Marlowe engaged in heartfelt conversations, their words floating into the night. The shared moments became like stones cast into the river, creating ripples of connection that extended far beyond the immediate. Liam and Marlowe revealed the simplicity of the moment, finding joy in the connection they shared and the beauty of the Parisian night. As the midnight hour approached, Liam and Marlowe decided to conclude their unforgettable night in the heart of Paris. They retraced their steps through the charming streets, hand in hand, with the echoes of laughter and shared moments lingering in the air. Returning to their home, the familiar surroundings welcomed them with a sense of warmth and familiarity. The soft glow of their living space, adorned with memories from their travels and shared experiences, felt like a sanctuary. The evening had been a symphony of love, and now it was time for the final notes to be played. Once inside, Liam and Marlowe embraced the quietude of their home. The comfort of familiar spaces and the shared energy of the night created a cocoon of intimacy. They settled into the cosiness of their living room, the soft lighting casting a gentle ambiance. Cuddling close, Liam and Marlowe found solace in each other's arms. The love that had flourished beneath the Eiffel Tower and along the Seine River now enveloped them like a tender embrace. The chill of the Parisian night was replaced by the warmth of their connection. Wrapped in the soft blankets of their shared experiences, they indulged in the simple joy of being close. The room was filled with the quiet sounds of whispered conversations, shared laughter, and the occasional exchange of affectionate glances. The night was a tapestry woven with threads of love, laughter, and the magic of shared moments. As they snuggled on the couch, Liam and Marlowe relished the closeness that only deepened with each passing moment. The city outside may have been bustling with its own rhythm, but within the walls of their home, time seemed to stand still. Every gaze, every touch, spoke volumes of the connection they shared. Their hearts beat in unison, a rhythmic melody that resonated with the memories of the night. The Eiffel Tower's lights may have dimmed, and the Seine River continued its gentle flow, but the love that Liam and Marlowe nurtured in their home remained vibrant and alive. As they drifted into a peaceful slumber, still wrapped in each other's embrace, Liam and Marlowe carried the essence of the starlit night and the romance of Paris into the realm of dreams.

Thirteen

Liam cherished Marlowe deeply, his love for her surpassing anything else in his life. Sensing that the time was ripe to propose, he arrived at the office earlier than usual, driven by a determination to complete his tasks ahead of schedule. Though not prompted by any official summons, Liam diligently piled up his workload, sending emails to his team and efficiently implementing major projects. Amidst his work, a brilliant idea struck him while browsing the internet. Aware of Marlowe's penchant for romance novels and his own talent for poetry, Liam decided to propose in a way that would resonate with her heart. Crafting a heartfelt poem, he inscribed the verses on a piece of paper and secured two novels Marlowe had longed to read. Liam's creative flair came into play as he carefully carved out a rectangle within one of the books to house the beautiful surprise he had in mind. Leaving no detail to chance, Liam ventured to a luxurious jewellery shop to acquire an exquisite Blue diamond ring for Marlowe. Though the expense was considerable, he believed the investment was justified by the profound significance of the moment. Having meticulously planned every detail, Liam orchestrated a surprise under the guise of a business trip. He called Marlowe, instructing her to pack their belongings for the supposed journey. Meanwhile, he hurriedly returned home, honked the car horn, and swiftly gathered their essentials, stowing them away in the car's trunk.

Their destination, an outskirts location, held the promise of unexpected turns in their lives. Embarking on a road trip, Liam and Marlowe revelled in the journey's unfolding surprises. As fatigue set in for Liam, Marlowe seamlessly assumed the role of the driver, and they exchanged places behind the wheel, seamlessly navigating the roads that led to a destination filled with love, anticipation, and a life-changing proposal waiting to unfurl. Upon reaching the outskirts location, Marlowe couldn't help but question Liam about the unexpected business trip and the mysterious itinerary. Liam, however, skillfully deflected her inquiries with a series of excuses, maintaining an air of secrecy around the surprise he had meticulously planned. A luxurious bungalow awaited them near a racing track, and the couple was warmly welcomed upon their arrival. To add to the intrigue, they were guided to an old car museum, a haven for vintage automotive treasures. As Marlowe marvelled at the engines she had only read about in novels, the atmosphere seemed almost dreamlike. As they explored the museum, Marlowe's excitement filled the air with awe. Liam, wearing a mysterious smile, discreetly stepped away. Suddenly, the lights dimmed, leaving only a spotlight guiding Marlowe's way. Following the illuminated path, Marlowe reached a spot where a key and a handwritten note awaited her. The note instructed Marlowe to exit the museum and take a seat behind the wheel of a particular car, urging her to drive it to the nearby track. Intrigued yet somewhat anxious, Marlowe called out for Liam, but there was no response. It felt as if he had vanished, leaving her in a state of confusion and anticipation. Undeterred, Marlowe decided to follow the instructions on the note. Exiting the museum, she found the designated car waiting for her. The engine roared to life as she settled into the driver's seat. The headlights pierced through the darkness as Marlowe cautiously drove towards the racing track, her curiosity and uncertainty growing with each passing moment. As Marlowe navigated the car onto the racing track, a flood of emotions overcame her when she spotted another sports car waiting in the dimly lit area. Coming to a stop, she noticed yet another note placed on the dashboard, instructing her to drive this new car on the racing track. With a mix of excitement and nervousness, Marlowe shifted behind the wheel of the second sports car. The engine roared to life, revealing it to be a powerful V12 Twin Turbo. Despite her initial nerves, a wave of exhilaration washed over her as she revved the engine, eager to experience the thrill of driving. She accelerated down the track, reaching speeds that added to the adrenaline coursing through her veins. After covering a distance of 8km, she noticed another car ahead, its headlights cutting through the darkness and casting a beam on the path before her. Marlowe slowed down as she approached the vehicle, her senses heightened and a touch of fear creeping in. With a tremor in her voice, she called out, "Who's there?" but received no response. Attempting to illuminate the surroundings with her phone's flashlight, Marlowe found visibility to be limited. Proceeding with caution, she continued along the track. To her relief, she discovered another note left on the windshield of the mysterious car. Pulling the wiper, Marlowe read the note, which finally revealed the next step. She was instructed to open the glove box and retrieve a book that had been carefully placed inside. The air was thick with anticipation as Marlowe followed the instructions, unfolding the layers of mystery that Liam had artfully crafted for her. Upon opening the glove box, Marlowe's eyes widened with delight as she beheld the book she had longed for. A surge of happiness filled her, and the mystery that had surrounded her night took a joyful turn. The racing track suddenly lit up, revealing a professional driver ready to showcase the art of drifting. As the skilled driver expertly manoeuvred the car in smooth, controlled drifts, Marlowe watched in awe. The tension and nerves that had initially gripped her gave way to a sense of relaxation. She carefully placed the coveted book aside, took hold of the wheel, and eagerly stepped into the driver's seat. With Liam as her passenger, Marlowe skillfully navigated the car through the twists and turns of the track. She slid through each curve, feeling the exhilaration of the racing experience. The roaring engine echoed the beating of her heart as she fully embraced the challenge. As Marlowe successfully completed the track, she arrived at the finish line where Liam was waiting. He hugged her tightly, playing the part of someone who had no knowledge of the evening's surprises. Marlowe, still bubbling with excitement, couldn't contain herself and explained every twist and turn of the unexpected adventure. Amused by Marlowe's enthusiasm, Liam confessed to orchestrating the entire plan. Marlowe laughed at the realisation that she had been denied the chance to read the book earlier, only for it to become a pivotal part of the surprise. Liam then directed the car to a secluded hill where interference faded away, leaving only Marlowe, Liam, and the open night sky. In the quiet solitude of the hill, Marlowe and Liam found themselves surrounded by a breathtaking view. The stars above sparkled, casting a gentle glow on the unfolding scene. Here, amidst the peacefulness, they could finally savour the moment they had shared, the surprises, and the love that had brought them to this beautiful hilltop. Eager to dive into the long-awaited book, Marlowe's excitement heightened as she finally started reading. The midnight sky provided the perfect backdrop as they reclined in the car, gazing at the twinkling stars. Page after page, Marlowe delved into the narrative, captivated by the story unfolding in her hands. As she turned the pages, she stumbled upon a particular page with a cutout, revealing a hidden compartment. To her astonishment, nestled within the cutout was a ring. Liam, seizing the opportune moment, was already on one knee, the ambiance around them echoing with a sense of hope and anticipation. Overwhelmed with emotion, Marlowe stood up and carefully retrieved the ring from its secret enclave. Tears of happiness welled in her eyes as she opened the car door and stepped outside. Liam, with the ring box in hand, knelt against the picturesque backdrop of mountains, creating a scene straight out of a dream. Marlowe handed the ring to Liam, who then began to recite the poem he had composed for her

"Beneath the stars, our love takes flight,
In tender whispers of the night.
With ring in hand, I humbly kneel,
A lifetime's promise, let's make it real.
Moonlit sky, witness to our embrace,
A question lingers, hearts set to race.
In this moment, love's sweet decree,
Will you be forever mine, eternally free?"

In a heartfelt moment, he posed the question, "Will you choose to be the sole love of my life for all eternity?" Marlowe, overcome with emotion, could only shake her head in amazement. Liam gently placed the ring on her finger, sealing the promise they shared. As if nature itself joined in their celebration, fireworks erupted in the night sky, casting a dazzling display of colours against the mountainous silhouette. In the midst of the crackling fireworks, Marlowe and Liam stood together, their hearts intertwined with the beauty of the moment. As Liam gently placed the ring on Marlowe's finger, sealing their commitment, Marlowe was overcome with joy. She leaned in, kissing Liam tenderly, her eyes sparkling with gratitude and love. Admiring the ring, she exclaimed about its beauty, marvelling at the craftsmanship. Curiosity sparkled in Marlowe's eyes as she inquired about the ring's price. However, Liam's response carried a depth that transcended monetary values. He looked into her eyes and softly said, "Marlowe, the cost is irrelevant. What holds significance is you, and I am ready to acquire anything that brings forth your smile." Marlowe, touched by Liam's sentiment, felt a warmth in her heart. In that moment, it became clear that the significance of the ring went beyond its material worth. Liam's words resonated with a commitment that surpassed the tangible, emphasising the priceless value of their shared happiness and the depth of their connection. As they stood beneath the shimmering fireworks, Locked in the magic of their forever commitment, Liam and Marlowe basked in the afterglow of the romantic proposal. However, Liam had one more surprise up his sleeve to elevate the enchantment of the evening. As they descended from the mountainous backdrop, they found themselves by a river flowing gently. A candlelit dinner awaited them, with the soft strains of a violin playing in the background, casting a spell of romance in the air. Marlowe, utterly amazed, couldn't contain her astonishment and joy. "Did you plan all this?" she asked Liam, her eyes reflecting a mix of surprise and admiration.

Liam, smiling, admitted, "Yes, I did. I'm sorry for the little white lie, but this was the plan all along." The flickering candlelight danced on the river's surface as they sat down to share a meal beneath the starry sky. The melody of the violin echoed through the night, harmonising with the symphony of their love. Liam's thoughtful surprises continued to unfold, creating an evening that surpassed any dream Marlowe could have envisioned. As they clinked glasses, Liam and Marlowe embraced the beauty of the moment, celebrating not only the beginning of their journey as an engaged couple but also the love that had paved the way for such magical memories. The dinner menu was a carefully curated selection of Marlowe's favourite dishes, each presented with artistic flair. Aromatic candles illuminated the scene, casting a warm glow on the table adorned with delicate flowers and elegant tableware. The sound of the flowing river provided a natural melody, complementing the soft strains of the violin in the background. To begin, a light and refreshing Caprese salad featured plump tomatoes, fresh mozzarella, and vibrant basil leaves, drizzled with a balsamic reduction that added a touch of sweetness. The flavours danced on their palates, setting the stage for the culinary journey ahead. The main course featured a succulent grilled salmon fillet, perfectly seasoned and accompanied by a medley of roasted vegetables. The salmon, cooked to perfection, flaked delicately beneath the touch of the fork, while the roasted vegetables provided a colourful and flavorful accompaniment. As the evening unfolded, the aroma of garlic-infused mashed potatoes wafted through the air, serving as a decadent side dish. The creamy texture and rich flavours added a comforting element to the meal, creating a symphony of tastes that delighted the senses.

To conclude the dinner on a sweet note, a delectable tiramisu was served. Layers of espresso-soaked ladyfingers and velvety mascarpone were expertly crafted, creating a dessert that was both indulgent and satisfying. The sweetness lingered on their taste buds, a perfect ending to a night filled with love, surprises, and the promise of a shared forever. As they savoured each bite, Liam and Marlowe couldn't help but marvel at the thought and effort Liam had put into creating this enchanting dinner by the riverside. The combination of exquisite flavours, the serene ambiance, and the backdrop of the flowing river made this meal not only a celebration of their engagement but also a feast for the heart and soul. As Marlowe indulged in the delightful flavours of the meticulously prepared dinner, the enchanting ambiance heightened her appreciation for the thought and effort Liam had put into the evening. The riverside setting, the gentle melodies of the violin, and the delectable dishes all contributed to a magical experience. With each bite and every shared glance, Marlowe's heart swelled with gratitude and love. Between courses, she couldn't help but express her overwhelming joy. "This is beyond amazing, Liam. I never expected such a beautiful and romantic proposal," Marlowe remarked, her eyes sparkling with delight.

Liam, pleased to see Marlowe's happiness, smiled warmly. "I'm glad you love it. You deserve nothing but the best," he replied, his gaze reflecting the depth of his affection. As the night unfolded, Marlowe couldn't help but feel that this was the best proposal she could have ever imagined. The combination of surprises, the breathtaking scenery, and the heartfelt moments shared with Liam created an evening that surpassed her wildest dreams. She cherished every detail, recognizing the effort and love Liam had poured into making it a night to remember. With the sound of the river as a soothing backdrop, Marlowe and Liam continued to savour the moments, immersed in the glow of their engagement. After the magical dinner by the riverside, Liam and Marlowe embarked on the serene drive back to their bungalow. The night air was cool, carrying with it the lingering echoes of the romantic melodies and the laughter they had shared. The winding roads led them through the quiet countryside, adding a sense of peacefulness to the journey. Inside the car, a comfortable silence enveloped them, allowing the magic of the night to linger. The engagement ring sparkled on Marlowe's finger, a constant reminder of the beautiful commitment they had made to each other. As they approached the bungalow, its warm lights beckoned them home. The familiar sight was now infused with the newfound significance of the evening. The crickets chirped softly in the background, creating a symphony that accompanied their thoughts. Once they reached the bungalow, Liam parked the car, and they stepped out into the still night. The air was filled with the fragrance of the surrounding nature, creating an ambiance of peace and contentment. Hand in hand, they entered the bungalow, where the memories of the night continued to unfold. The room seemed to embrace the happiness that had filled their hearts. Marlowe couldn't help but reflect on the surreal beauty of the evening, and Liam, too, found joy in seeing her so elated.The bungalow became a haven of love, where the echoes of their laughter and the promises made under the starry sky would forever resonate. Liam and Marlowe allowed the night to draw its curtains, looking forward to the countless adventures that awaited them as they embarked on this new chapter of their lives.

Fourteen

The next morning, the soft glow of sunlight streamed into the bungalow, gently waking Marlowe and Liam. As they stepped into the living area, a delightful aroma led them to a table adorned with a scrumptious breakfast. Freshly baked pastries, tropical fruits, and aromatic coffee awaited them, reflecting the care and attention to detail that had become a hallmark of their stay. After savouring the delicious breakfast, Marlowe and Liam were pleasantly surprised when the bungalow staff offered them a luxurious spa experience. A relaxing bath adorned with fragrant petals awaited them, and the couple, already in sync with the enchantment of the weekend, decided to bathe together. The warmth of the water, coupled with the peacefulness of the surroundings, created a serene and intimate atmosphere. As they shared laughter and tender moments, it became a soothing prelude to the day that awaited them. Post their refreshing bath, another surprise awaited Marlowe and Liam. Two top-notch cars were presented to them, sleek machines that promised an exhilarating experience on the racing track. Grinning with excitement, they donned helmets and slid into the driver's seats. Guided by experienced instructors, they navigated the track with speed, mastering the curves and straights. Every turn, every acceleration, and every brake manoeuvre added to the thrill of the experience. Despite the adrenaline rush, safety measures were paramount, ensuring a perfect blend of excitement and security. As they revved the engines and raced down the track, The racing track echoed with the thunderous roar of engines as Marlowe and Liam sped through the twists and turns, their cars slicing through the air with precision and grace. The excitement on the track was palpable, and the friendly competition between the engaged couple added an extra layer of exhilaration. As they navigated the circuit, Marlowe's skills behind the wheel shone brightly. With each curve, she displayed finesse, taking on the challenges of the track with confidence. The instructors observed her techniques and commended her on the seamless manoeuvres. Liam, though competitive, couldn't help but admire Marlowe's prowess on the track. The corners seemed to yield to her command, and the straightaways showcased the power and control she wielded over the car. The track became a canvas, and Marlowe, the skilled artist, painted a masterpiece with every lap. The race intensified, and as they approached the finish line, it became evident that Marlowe had claimed victory. The chequered flag waved triumphantly, marking her as the winner of the friendly competition. Cheers erupted from the sidelines, and even Liam couldn't suppress a grin, proud of Marlowe's achievement. After the exhilarating race, Marlowe and Liam shared a celebratory moment on the track. They exchanged laughter, high-fives, and a sweet victory kiss, sealing the joyous memory of the race. The experience not only brought an adrenaline rush but also strengthened the bond between them. In that shared victory, Marlowe and Liam discovered the thrill of conquering challenges together, a preview of the victories and joys they would celebrate throughout their journey as a couple. After the exhilarating victory on the racing track, Marlowe and Liam continued their day with a sense of shared accomplishment. The bungalow staff, aware of their preferences, had arranged a private picnic overlooking a scenic spot near the river. A spread of gourmet delights awaited them, and they spent the afternoon relishing delicious food and each other's company. With a sense of contentment and a touch of playfulness, they explored the picturesque surroundings. Strolling hand in hand, they revelled in the beauty of nature and the shared moments that had filled their weekend with joy. The river, the gentle breeze, and the rustling leaves seemed to dance in harmony, creating a symphony of peace and love. As the day unfolded, the couple indulged in a couple's massage, allowing the skilled hands of the spa therapists to melt away any residual tension from the day's adventures. The soothing ambiance and the fragrant aromas added to the overall feeling of relaxation. In the evening, they decided to explore a nearby quaint town, immersing themselves in its charm. They wandered through narrow streets lined with artisan shops, enjoyed a cosy dinner at a local restaurant, and shared laughter over ice cream from a charming dessert shop. As the night descended, bringing a blanket of stars above, Marlowe and Liam made their way back to the bungalow. With hearts full of cherished memories, they packed their belongings, ready to return to their home. In the moments before they left, they stood hand in hand, soaking in the serene ambiance of the bungalow. The echoes of laughter, the taste of victory, and the shared experiences painted a canvas of love that would forever adorn the walls of their shared history. When the time came to leave, Marlowe and Liam took one last glance at the place that had witnessed the magic of their engagement celebration. With a promise to return, they drove away under the moonlit sky. As Marlowe and Liam drove through the night, the winding roads seemed to echo the whispers of their shared laughter and the joyous moments they had experienced. The soft hum of the car's engine accompanied the gentle rustling of leaves, creating a soothing melody as they journeyed back home. Inside the car, the air was filled with a comfortable silence, interspersed with occasional glances and smiles that spoke volumes. The engagement ring sparkled on Marlowe's finger, a symbol of the promises made and the adventures yet to unfold. The journey back became a reflection of the weekend, a blend of excitement, peacefulness, and the anticipation of a future filled with love. Marlowe, gazing out of the window, felt a profound sense of happiness and contentment. Liam, focused on the road ahead, couldn't help but steal glances at Marlowe, grateful for the shared experiences that had strengthened their connection. As they approached their home, the familiar surroundings welcomed them back. The quietude of the night enveloped them, creating a serene atmosphere. Marlowe and Liam, hand in hand, entered their home, bringing with them the echoes of the special weekend. In the glow of the soft lighting, they found comfort in each other's presence. Marlowe, feeling a mixture of excitement and calm, couldn't help but express her gratitude to Liam for the unforgettable weekend. Liam, with a tender smile, assured her that there were many more adventures to come. They spent the remaining hours of the night unpacking and settling back into the routine of home. As they curled up together, they relived the moments that had made the weekend extraordinary. The engagement ring glittered in the moonlight, a symbol of their commitment and the love that bound them together. As the night unfolded, Marlowe and Liam drifted into a peaceful sleep, cradled by the warmth of their shared journey. The weekend had marked the beginning of a beautiful chapter, and the promise of a lifetime of love and adventures awaited the couple as they embarked on this remarkable journey together. Back in the familiar routine of daily life, Marlowe and Liam seamlessly transitioned from the enchanting weekend to their professional responsibilities. The echoes of their engagement lingered in the background, creating a subtle undercurrent of happiness that accompanied them to the workplace. As they reported back to the office, colleagues noticed the radiant glow on Marlowe's face and the sparkling ring on her finger. The inquisitive glances and curious whispers from coworkers couldn't be ignored. Marlowe, aware of the company's policy on relationships among colleagues, decided to keep the engagement discreet for the time being. Whenever questioned about the ring, Marlowe skillfully crafted excuses, citing it as a gift from a close friend or a family heirloom. She navigated these conversations with grace and a charming smile, managing to divert attention while maintaining an air of mystery. Liam, understanding the need for discretion, played along with the charade, blending seamlessly into the office routine. They bound by their commitment to each other, found joy in the shared glances and secret smiles. The workplace became a stage for their clandestine connection, adding an element of excitement to their otherwise routine tasks. Despite the need for discretion, Marlowe and Liam continued to flourish both personally and professionally. Their bond, strengthened by shared experiences and mutual support, became an anchor in the midst of the everyday hustle and bustle. Marlowe and Liam knew that their love story, though hidden for now, was destined to unfold in its own time. The office corridors may have been filled with questions, but the couple remained united, ready to face whatever challenges lay ahead on their shared journey.

The news of Marlowe and Liam's engagement, which had been kept discreet within the office, reached the ears of the board members. In response, the board called for a meeting, summoning Marlowe and Liam to address the matter. The atmosphere in the room carried a sense of formality, with stern faces observing the couple as they entered.

Seated across from the board, Marlowe and Liam faced a barrage of questions about their relationship and the implications it might have on their professional roles. The board members expressed concerns about potential conflicts of interest, company policies, and the impact on their respective responsibilities. However, Marlowe and Liam, standing united, responded with a calm and unwavering determination. They acknowledged the concerns raised by the board but emphasised that their commitment to each other did not compromise their dedication to their work. In a firm yet respectful tone, they stated that love was not a hindrance to professionalism, and their engagement did not affect their competence or commitment. Marlowe, with a composed demeanour, articulated, "If our relationship is perceived as an issue, we're willing to step aside from our current roles. However, we won't step away from each other. Love is not a distraction but a source of strength that fuels our dedication to our personal and professional lives." Liam, echoing Marlowe's sentiments, added, "We believe in transparency and honesty. We won't hide our love, but we also won't let it interfere with our responsibilities. If the board deems our engagement inappropriate, we'll accept the consequences, but we won't compromise on our commitment to each other." The board, though initially stern, was taken aback by the couple's resolute stance. After a moment of contemplation, the atmosphere softened. The chairperson of the board finally spoke, "We appreciate your honesty and commitment. We'll take your words into consideration and discuss the matter further. For now, continue your roles as usual." Marlowe and Liam left the meeting with a mix of relief and determination. Their love had been put to the test, and they emerged stronger, ready to face whatever challenges lay ahead. The board's decision would unfold in due time, but Marlowe and Liam remained steadfast in their belief that love and professionalism could coexist harmoniously. In a surprising turn of events, the board members reconvened to deliberate on the matter of Marlowe and Liam's engagement. After careful consideration, they realised the need for a reevaluation of the company's policies regarding relationships among employees. The couple's steadfast commitment to both their personal and professional lives had left a profound impact on the board. In an official announcement, the board expressed their regret for the outdated policy that had initially caused concern. They acknowledged the changing dynamics of the modern workplace and recognized that fostering an inclusive and supportive environment was crucial for the well-being of their employees. Liam and Marlowe, grateful for the board's willingness to adapt, felt a sense of vindication for their honesty and perseverance. The board assured them that their engagement would no longer be perceived as a hindrance to their professional roles, and the company would work towards creating an environment that celebrated diversity and personal relationships. The policy change was not only a victory for Marlowe and Liam but also a milestone for the entire company. It reflected a commitment to progress, inclusivity, and understanding the evolving needs of its workforce. Marlowe and Liam continued their roles with renewed confidence, knowing that their love story had not only weathered a storm but had also played a part in bringing about positive change. The workplace, once marked by discreet glances and hidden smiles, now embraced their relationship openly. The couple's journey together continued, not just as a personal adventure, but also as contributors to a workplace culture that valued authenticity and the harmonious integration of personal and professional lives. Embracing the positive shift in company policy, Marlowe and Liam found themselves at the forefront of a workplace transformation. The newfound openness allowed them to navigate their professional roles with greater ease and authenticity. No longer burdened by the need for secrecy, their shared moments became a source of inspiration for others. As the weeks passed, the board's commitment to fostering a supportive workplace culture became evident. The company organised events and workshops aimed at promoting diversity, inclusion, and work-life balance. The corporate atmosphere transformed into a more compassionate and understanding environment, where personal relationships were celebrated rather than discouraged. Marlowe and Liam continued to excel in their respective roles, and their dedication to both their personal and professional lives became a model for others. The workplace, once marked by rigid policies, now echoed with the harmonious integration of work and personal life. The couple's influence reached beyond the office walls. External recognition followed as the company received accolades for its commitment to fostering an inclusive and supportive workplace. Marlowe and Liam, once faced with challenges, had become agents of positive change. As they attended company events and gatherings together, the couple felt a sense of pride in the impact they had made.

Fifteen

Eager to share their joyous news with their families, Marlowe and Liam embarked on the task of explaining their engagement. Although they were met with varying reactions, the couple was determined to create a bridge between their respective worlds. Liam, being close to his mother, chose to share the news with her first. He arranged a casual gathering at his home, creating a warm and welcoming atmosphere. Liam's mother, filled with excitement, was overjoyed to hear about her son's engagement. She expressed her happiness, embracing the idea of Marlowe becoming a part of their family. Meanwhile, Marlowe had already been introduced to the concept of Liam's family dynamics. Liam had shared stories and details about his father, who, for various reasons, could not be present at the gathering. Understanding the complexities involved, Marlowe respected Liam's decision and chose not to press the matter further. On the day of the gathering, Liam's mother welcomed Marlowe with open arms. The two women quickly formed a connection, sharing stories and laughter, making the atmosphere warm and inviting. The absence of Liam's father was acknowledged with sensitivity, and the focus remained on celebrating the union of two families. As the evening unfolded, Liam's mother expressed her admiration for Marlowe and the love she saw between the couple. She reassured Marlowe that, despite the circumstances, she was thrilled to welcome her into the family. Marlowe, touched by the genuine warmth, felt a sense of belonging that transcended any initial reservations.

Liam and Marlowe, united in their commitment to each other, navigated the complexities of blending their families with grace and understanding. The gathering became a symbol of the love and acceptance that could bridge any gaps, fostering an environment where familial bonds could grow. As the families gathered to celebrate Marlowe and Liam's engagement, the atmosphere was filled with joy, laughter, and the promise of new beginnings. The families, each with their unique stories and backgrounds, came together to discuss the union that would bring them even closer. Liam's mother, being the gracious host, initiated conversations that revolved around shared interests, values, and traditions. Marlowe's family, eager to get to know Liam's side, enthusiastically participated in discussions that ranged from family traditions to future plans for the engaged couple. Stories were shared, anecdotes exchanged, and laughter echoed through the room as the families found common ground. Marlowe's parents, having heard about Liam's father from their daughter, approached the topic with sensitivity, ensuring that the atmosphere remained respectful and understanding. The engaged couple played an essential role in facilitating the conversations, helping the families connect over shared experiences and aspirations. Discussions about cultural nuances, family customs, and expectations for the upcoming wedding were approached with openness and flexibility. While Liam's mother shared fond memories of Liam's childhood, Marlowe's parents spoke proudly of their daughter's achievements and the strong values instilled in her. The families found themselves bonding over a shared commitment to supporting Marlowe and Liam's journey. The absence of Liam's father was acknowledged, and Marlowe's family expressed their understanding and willingness to embrace him when the time was right. The gathering became a testament to the transformative power of love, bridging gaps and fostering connections that transcended individual histories. As the evening progressed, plans for the upcoming wedding were discussed, with both families actively participating in shaping the celebration. The families exchanged contact information, creating a network that would continue to grow as they navigated the exciting journey toward the union of Marlowe and Liam. The meeting concluded with a sense of unity, as the families embraced the idea of becoming interconnected through the upcoming wedding. Following the initial gathering, the families of Marlowe and Liam continued to build connections and strengthen their bonds through frequent calls and messages. The excitement surrounding the upcoming wedding provided a platform for collaborative planning, with everyone contributing ideas to shape a celebration that would truly reflect the unique union of the engaged couple. Group calls became a common occurrence, allowing both families to discuss various aspects of the wedding. Marlowe's parents and Liam's mother, now familiar voices on the other end of the line, exchanged ideas, shared anecdotes, and collaborated on decisions ranging from venue selection to cultural traditions that would be incorporated into the ceremony. Messages flew back and forth, carrying the enthusiasm and anticipation of the families as they collectively envisioned the special day. The exchange of photos, wedding inspirations, and even virtual tours of potential venues helped bridge the physical distance between them, fostering a sense of togetherness despite being miles apart. Both families, motivated by a shared commitment to make the wedding a memorable occasion, actively participated in the planning process. Marlowe's mother, with her eye for detail, contributed suggestions for floral arrangements and decor, while Liam's mother shared insights on cultural rituals that could be woven into the ceremony. The collaborative efforts extended to selecting the menu, considering music choices, and coordinating attire to ensure a harmonious blend of both families' preferences. Despite the diverse backgrounds and traditions, a shared vision emerged-one that celebrated the union of Marlowe and Liam in a way that resonated with both families. The families, united by their love and support for the engaged couple, found common ground in the joyous anticipation of the upcoming celebration.The wedding preparations kicked into high gear as Marlowe and Liam, along with their families, delved into the exciting process of shopping for the bride and groom. The enchanting backdrop of Lake Como, Italy, set the stage for a celebration that promised to be as stunning as the love story it was commemorating. For Marlowe, the search for the perfect wedding attire was a journey filled with anticipation and joy. Together with her mother and close friends, she explored various bridal boutiques, poring over intricate lace patterns, luxurious fabrics, and elegant designs. The fitting sessions were moments of pure bliss, as Marlowe envisioned herself walking down the aisle in a gown that captured the essence of her love story. Liam, equally enthusiastic about the upcoming nuptials, embarked on his own quest for the ideal groom's attire. With the guidance of his mother and close confidantes, he explored classic and contemporary styles, ensuring that his ensemble would complement the picturesque surroundings of Lake Como. Fittings became opportunities for laughter and camaraderie as Liam envisioned standing at the altar, ready to embark on a new chapter of his life. The families, bridging geographical distances through technology, shared images and opinions on the chosen attire for the bride and groom. Virtual calls turned into mini fashion shows as Marlowe twirled in her wedding gown, and Liam showcased his impeccable suit. The shared excitement and anticipation strengthened the familial bonds, creating a sense of unity even in the midst of wedding preparations. As the wedding date approached, final fittings took place, and the attire for both Marlowe and Liam was carefully packed, ready to make the journey to Lake Como. The families, united in their shared commitment to creating a memorable celebration, worked tirelessly to ensure that every detail, from the attire to the decor, reflected the unique love story of the couple. The air was filled with excitement as Marlowe and Liam, with their families by their side, prepared to embark on a once-in-a-lifetime celebration in the breathtaking setting of Lake Como. The wedding attire, carefully chosen and infused with love, served as a proof to the merging of two lives, two families, and the beginning of a beautiful journey as Marlowe and Liam readied themselves for their dream wedding in Italy.

The venue, nestled against the stunning backdrop of the Italian lakes, was transformed into a haven of romance and enchantment. Floral arrangements in hues that echoed the natural beauty of Lake Como adorned every corner, creating an atmosphere of elegance and timeless charm. The families worked together to oversee the setup, ensuring that the venue reflected the love and commitment shared by Marlowe and Liam. Rehearsals and run-throughs added a touch of familiarity to the proceedings. The families, joined by close friends and well-wishers, practised their roles in the ceremony, making sure that every aspect unfolded seamlessly. Laughter and shared moments of anticipation filled the air as everyone involved felt the weight of the upcoming celebration. As the sun dipped below the horizon, casting a warm glow over Lake Como, the families gathered for a pre-wedding dinner filled with toasts, laughter, and heartfelt speeches. The shared joy and sense of unity became palpable, setting the tone for the extraordinary celebration that awaited Marlowe and Liam. The eve of the wedding saw the families coming together for a traditional rehearsal dinner.

Sixteen

On the day of Marlowe and Liam's wedding, the final location at Lake Como radiated with an ethereal beauty that seemed almost surreal. The early morning sun painted the sky with hues of pink and gold, casting a warm glow over the serene waters and lush surroundings. As guests arrived, they were greeted by the breathtaking scenery that framed the celebration-a union of love against the backdrop of one of Italy's most enchanting landscapes. The venue, meticulously adorned with flowers, captured the essence of romance. Delicate blooms in shades of ivory, blush, and soft greens adorned archways, aisle runners, and every corner of the outdoor ceremony space. The fragrance of fresh blossoms wafted through the air, creating an atmosphere of natural elegance that mirrored the love shared between Marlowe and Liam. A gracefully adorned arch marked the focal point of the ceremony space, overlooking the shimmering waters of Lake Como. Assembled with meticulous attention to detail, the arch became a symbol of unity, representing the merging of two lives and families on this momentous day. The seating arrangements, draped in flowing fabrics and adorned with floral accents, provided an intimate setting for the families and guests to witness the exchange of vows. Each carefully placed chair seemed to be an invitation to share in the joy and promise of Marlowe and Liam's union. The pathways leading to the ceremony space were lined with soft petals, creating a romantic walkway for the bridal party. The natural beauty of Lake Como seamlessly blended with the curated decor, enhancing the overall ambiance of the celebration. As Marlowe descended down the aisle, her radiant beauty illuminated by the soft morning light, the awe-inspiring surroundings added an extra layer of magic to the moment. Liam, awaiting his bride at the altar, looked on with a mix of anticipation and admiration, encapsulating the essence of two souls destined to be united. As Marlowe and Liam sealed their vows with a tender kiss, a moment of sheer magic unfolded at Lake Como. The serene atmosphere was suddenly electrified with a burst of vibrant colours that adorned the sky. The newlyweds' kiss seemed to set off a cascade of emotions, manifesting in a breathtaking display of fireworks that lit up the evening. The sky became a canvas painted with myriad hues-soft pinks, radiant blues, and shimmering golds. The explosions of colour mirrored the jubilation and joy resonating throughout the venue. The families and guests, still caught in the spell of the intimate ceremony, were now further enchanted by the kaleidoscopic symphony that unfolded above. The reflection of the fireworks danced on the tranquil waters of Lake Como, creating an enchanting spectacle that added a touch of magic to the celebration. The families, gathered to witness the union of Marlowe and Liam, found themselves immersed in a moment that transcended the ordinary, as the colours painted the sky in celebration of love. The explosive display of fireworks continued, each burst harmonising with the rhythm of the couple's heartbeat. Marlowe and Liam, surrounded by the brilliant spectacle, shared a gaze filled with gratitude and joy. The families, their faces illuminated by the colourful glow, revelled in the shared delight of this unexpected and magnificent celebration. The guests, too, were caught in the awe-inspiring moment, their cheers and applause blending with the crackling sounds of the fireworks. The different shades of colours created an ethereal atmosphere, turning the wedding celebration into a symphony of visual delight. As the final burst of fireworks painted the night sky, the families and guests stood in collective admiration of the beauty that unfolded before them. The lake, the mountains, and the sky seemed to converge in a moment of pure magic, encapsulating the essence of Marlowe and Liam's love story.

The families, now bathed in the afterglow of the colourful display, carried the memory of this enchanting celebration with them. The unexpected burst of fireworks became a symbol of the joy, unity, and the profound love that marked the union of Marlowe and Liam-a celebration that transcended the ordinary and unfolded against the backdrop of the captivating beauty of Lake Como. The evening at Lake Como unfolded like a dream, with the sun gracefully setting over the tranquil waters, casting a warm, golden glow upon the festivities. The reception venue, adorned with twinkling lights and elegantly arranged candlelit tables, became a haven of enchantment. Each detail was meticulously crafted, adding a touch of sophistication to the celebration. Guests immersed themselves in the joyous atmosphere, raising toasts to the newlyweds against the mesmerising backdrop of the illuminated lake. The air was filled with the tinkling sounds of laughter and clinking glasses, creating a symphony of celebration that echoed through the night. Under the canopy of the starlit sky, dance became the language of the evening. The families, now seamlessly intertwined through Marlowe and Liam's union, embraced the lively celebration. The dance floor became a stage where laughter, joy, and love merged in a harmonious rhythm. As the night progressed, the festivities unfolded like a kaleidoscope of emotions, painting memories that would linger in the hearts of all who attended. The families revelled in the culmination of months of meticulous planning, witnessing the beginning of a shared journey marked by love and unity. The final location at Lake Como, a testament to nature's beauty and thoughtful decor, provided the perfect stage for a wedding day that exceeded every expectation. As the families shared in the joy of Marlowe and Liam's love story, they found themselves connected through this unforgettable celebration. The magical setting mirrored the enchantment of the newlyweds' union, weaving a tapestry of memories that would be cherished for a lifetime. The night continued with laughter, dance, and the gentle hum of conversations under the starlit sky. Lake Como, with its serene waters and picturesque surroundings, became the canvas for an extraordinary celebration-one that celebrated not only the union of Marlowe and Liam but also the enduring bonds of family and the promise of a future filled with love and shared adventures. As the night at Lake Como approached its end, the enchanting celebration began to wind down, leaving lingering echoes of joy and love in the hearts of all who attended. The families, now connected through the magic of Marlowe and Liam's union, shared heartfelt embraces and warm wishes as they bid farewell to the extraordinary day. The twinkling lights that adorned the reception venue continued to cast a soft glow, creating a magical ambiance that reflected the love and unity celebrated throughout the evening. Guests, carrying the memories of laughter, dance, and toasts, departed with a sense of fulfilment, knowing they had been part of a truly special moment. Marlowe and Liam, surrounded by the remnants of the festivities, stood hand in hand, gazing at the illuminated lake and the starlit sky. The final location at Lake Como, once a stage for their love story, now witnessed the quiet beauty of the night settling in. As the families dispersed, the newlyweds embraced the peacefulness of the moment-a moment that marked not just the end of a day but the beginning of a shared journey. They took a leisurely stroll, hand in hand, along the shores of Lake Como, reflecting on the love, support, and joy that filled their hearts. The night, woven with the threads of enchantment, came to a close with the promise of a beautiful sunrise to follow. Marlowe and Liam, now united in marriage, embarked on a new chapter of their lives, carrying the warmth of Lake Como's magic with them. And so, beneath the starlit sky, the celebration concluded-a celebration that transcended the ordinary, leaving behind a tapestry of cherished moments that would forever be etched in the hearts of all who witnessed the union of Marlowe and Liam at the breathtaking Lake Como.

Acknowledgement

I extend my heartfelt gratitude to the many individuals who have supported me throughout this incredible journey of writing and publishing my book. Without their unwavering encouragement, guidance, and belief in my abilities, this endeavour would not have been possible.

First and foremost, I would like to express my deepest appreciation to my family. Your endless love, patience, and understanding have been the pillars of my strength. Thank you for always encouraging me to pursue my passions and for instilling in me the value of hard work and determination.

I am indebted to the team at Croiretre, and The Webasing, whose collective effort and dedication have made this book a reality. Your expertise and commitment to excellence have been truly inspiring. Thank you for believing in my vision and for working tirelessly to bring it to fruition.I would like to express my gratitude to the editors and proofreaders who have contributed their time and expertise to refine the manuscript. Your meticulous attention to detail and insightful suggestions have elevated the quality of this book.

Finally, I want to thank all those who have played a part, big or small, in shaping my journey as a writer or as an entrepreneur. Your belief in my abilities has fueled my passion and motivated me to strive for excellence.

To each and every individual who has touched my life and contributed to this book, please accept my sincerest gratitude. Your presence in my journey is cherished and your support is deeply valued.

Infallible Two: Starlit Love

Infallible Two: Starlit Love is a riveting story about unplanned interactions and the strength of love that overcomes all obstacles. Trevor Cartier, still buzzing after the energetic party, meets Delacey Dunne, an elusive woman. After being brought together by fate, they set off on an epic voyage of sharing moments, insecurities, and undeniable attraction. As their bond grows stronger, they realize that their chance encounter was not a coincidence but rather the beginning of a love story foretold by the stars. In a world where fate appears inevitable, Trevor and Delacey's relationship is a testament that true love transcends all limits.

Unerring Two: Longing And Heartcapes

Trevor's relentless pursuit of Delacey mirrors the desperation of a man consumed by longing. Every unturned stone and uncharted avenue deepens his determination to reunite with her, painting a vivid picture of his devotion against the canvas of uncertainty. As Delacey and Mateo's journey unfolds, they find themselves traversing both physical landscapes and the landscapes of their own hearts. The echoes of their past resonate with every step, casting shadows on their present choices and prompting them to contemplate the roads they have taken. Amidst the twists and turns of this novel's rich tapestry, themes of love, loss, and the resilience of the human spirit come to the forefront.